BOYS, BROTHERS AND JELLY-BELLY DANCING

"Oh, and Ally – there's something else," Billy whispered.

"What?" I quizzed him, finding myself whispering too – who knows why, since the only pair of ears listening in to my end of the conversation belonged to a cat that wasn't Colin, who was gently snorey-purring through the bannisters behind me on the stairs.

"Can't tell you now. Tell you when I see you tomorrow night."

"Aw, come on – that's not fair! You've got to give me a little clue at least!" I teased him.

"OK," he hissed, sounding strangely wobbly. "It's just that I think ... I think I'm in love!"

Billy in love? For real? For *real* real? Not just fancying someone?

Well, blow me down with a whole *bunch* of feathers. This was serious. And weird. Actually, hearing his news right there? That's how I felt – seriously weird...

Karen McCombie's Scrumptious Books

Sadie ROCKS!

Happiness, and All That Stuff
Deep Joy, or Something Like It
It's All Good (In Your Dreams)
Smile! It's Meant to be Fun

ALLY'S WORLD

Collect all 16 fabulous titles!

Stella Etc.

7 sunshiney, seasidey, unmissable books

And her novels
Marshmallow Magic and the Wild Rose Rouge
An Urgent Message of Wowness

Karen McCombie

BOYS, BROTHERS AND JELLY-BELLY DANCING

Welcome to the weird and wonderful world of Ally Love, age 13…

ALLY'S WORLD

■SCHOLASTIC

For Miss Lou —

My shimmy-tastic buddy

Scholastic Children's Books
An imprint of Scholastic Ltd
Euston House, 24 Eversholt Street
London, NW1 1DB, UK
Registered office: Westfield Road, Southam, Warwickshire, CV47 0RA
SCHOLASTIC and associated logos are trademarks and/or registered
trademarks of Scholastic Inc.

First published in the UK by Scholastic Ltd, 2002
This edition published in the UK by Scholastic Ltd, 2011

Text copyright © Karen McCombie, 2002
The right of Karen McCombie to be identified as the author
of this work has been asserted by her.

ISBN 978 1407 11785 0

Printed in the UK by CPI Bookmarque, Croydon, Surrey.
Papers used by Scholastic Children's Books are made from
wood grown in sustainable forests.

1 3 5 7 9 10 8 6 4 2

www.scholastic.co.uk/zone

Contents

PROLOGUE

Dear Mum,

One word: boys.

Why didn't you ever tell me how confused they make you feel? I don't mean fancying them or dating them (I know *that*'s confusing), but just boys in general. Even just trying to be *friends* with them gets confusing. It's like me and Billy recently – one minute he was being his usual nice, goof-ball self, the next he was driving me demented, and the next minute I was feeling all … well … *weird* about him.

Now? I suppose me and Billy are more or less back to normal, but I could really have done with you being around to help me sort my head out on that one. For a couple of weeks there, I wasn't sure if I wanted to kick him or – urgh – *kiss* him…

Yuck – quick, change the subject before I *barf*…

Well, one thing you *did* tell me about a long time ago was that it's OK to be rubbish at sports. I'm glad you gave me that bit of advice, because I'm *still* rubbish at sports, but it doesn't bother me any more. (You'll be pleased to know that I've passed on this nugget of wisdom to Tor, who managed to come in last in just about everything at his school sports day today. According to Grandma, who went along to watch, it was because he kept getting distracted by a dog in the crowd. It kept "smiling" at him, Tor told Grandma afterwards.*)

Anyhow, here's a bit of a surprise for you – maybe I'm not too hot at sports, but I have been trying to get fit recently, and it involves camels. Oh, and speaking of animals, I guess you'll need to hear all about Tor and the mouse poem, since it concerns you.

Confused yet? Well, OK, I'll shut up for now and get on with writing down what happened. But first I'll go and grab some nachos from the kitchen. Hey, I know they're fattening, but a few camels will soon burn a bunch of calories off...

Love you lots,

Ally

(your Love child No. 3)

* To be honest, I completely understand why it's more fun spending time smiling back at a friendly dog than risk falling flat on your face while thundering along inside a sack at high speed.

Chapter 1

OH, TO BE A "B"...

"Ally! Lemme in!" Tor yelped from the other side of the bathroom door.

"Five more minutes!" I shouted back.

It wasn't as if I was exactly enjoying my bath (the water was getting way too lukewarm – or luke*cold* for that matter), but right at that moment I was transfixed, marvelling at how my pretty-much-flat chest looked flatter than ever when I was lying back. From this angle, I looked like a cross between an ironing board and a *boy*.

But you know something? Even though I'm only an AA in bra size (hey, a *big* move on from the "zero" size I used to be not so long ago), and *even* though I regularly catch myself staring at my sisters' and friends' B+ efforts and wishing *I* had a couple of those, one thing you'd never find me doing is drooling over cosmetic surgery brochures and counting off the days till I'm eighteen and old enough for a boob job. Oh, no.

There are several reasons for that, including:

1) PAIN. Me and my sisters watched (and nearly puked over) a TV documentary on implants a while ago, and on it they showed an actual operation, where this girl had her boob cut open and then … *stuffed*. There was tons of blood and gloopy bits of fat that looked like *frog*spawn for goodness' sake, and NO ONE IS EVER DOING THAT TO ME. Specially if they expect to get paid for the privilege. Which brings me on to…

2) COST. Unless my dad starts selling diamond-encrusted bicycles in his shop instead of ordinary second-hand ones, he's never going to be able to afford to treat me to a boob job. And unless I found a morning paper-round that pays two hundred quid a week (know any?), I wouldn't be able to save up for one either. And if pain and lack or money wasn't enough, there's always…

3) FEAR. I've heard that implants can explode on planes. OK, so maybe it's just one of those urban myths (like baby alligators getting flushed down the toilet and turning into mutant monsters who trawl the sewers – *blee!*) but if it's true, well, having your boob explode in mid-air sounds really scary, as well as painful, and you sure wouldn't look too hot in a bikini after that. Speaking of fear, there's also…

4) MY GRANDMA. My grandma is one thousand

per cent against cosmetic surgery. I mean, she thinks it's absolutely fine and justified if your ears stick out so much they get caught in lift doors or something, but any more than that then she thinks people need their heads examined. Plus, when I moaned about the size of my non-existent chest to her one time before, she told me that boobs don't stop growing till girls are in their late teens, sometimes early twenties. Could you imagine if you asked some surgeon to pump you up a couple of sizes, and then went and grew bigger naturally too? You could end up a triple H and be in danger of toppling over every time you walked downhill. You'd have to wear a rucksack on your back permanently, just to balance you out.

"*Allllyyyyyyyy!!*"

"Be out in a couple of minutes!" I shouted back at my brother.

Nope, I decided, looking down through the water at my pathetic excuse for boobs, *I'll just have to go for the Wonderbra option if it ever bothers me too much.*

And with that, I put my hands on either side of my size AAs and squished them together, which was actually deeply unattractive. But not as unattractive as something *else* that had just appeared on the horizon...

I gasped at the big, blobby thing that had just risen out of the foamy bubbles: was it an over-inflated pink balloon? Was it a basking whale? Gingerly, I lifted my dripping hand out of the bathwater and tentatively gave The Thing a prod with my finger. It wobbled. It wobbled like a jelly. Omigod. I, Ally Love, had – eek! – a jelly belly.

That was so unfair! How could that have happened? I was really fit! (Well, I walked the dogs now and then.) I ate well! (Um, apart from the occasional bag or six of crisps, of course.)

"*Allllyyyyyyy!*"

"*What*?!" I replied irritably to the whiny voice out on the landing. (Although I wasn't really bugged by my brother, just by the jelly belly that was sitting staring back at me.)

Tor didn't answer. He just knocked and knocked and knocked some more, like a demented woodpecker.

Sploshing out of the bath, I grabbed my white towelling bathrobe, hauled it on and yanked the door open.

"What's the big rush?" I asked, looking down at his earnest face.

I should have guessed from the way he was standing, I suppose. With one hand held up to tap on the door and his legs wrapped weirdly around one another, he looked like a woodpecker doing an advanced yoga position.

"Got to go NOW!" he yelped, pushing past me.

I found myself grinning and then stopped. There was no point laughing at Tor for the funny way he'd looked. I mean, all that was wrong with him was that he was desperate for a wee.

Whereas me, with my no-boobs and jelly belly … well, I must have looked like a giant pear in a dressing gown.

And that, in case you hadn't worked it out, is *so* not a good look…

Chapter 2

CRISPS OF DESTINY...

"Ally," said Kyra, flicking her eyes up and down me, "what exactly are you *wearing*?"

It was a pretty nice day, so me, Sandie and Kyra had come up to Alexandra Palace after school had finished this Friday afternoon, and sprawled ourselves on the grass, ready to yak about this, that and not very much, really.

"School uniform?" I shrugged, pretending I didn't get what Kyra meant.

"Oh, yeah? But what are you wearing that stupid Arran jumper for? Are you planning an expedition up the west face of Everest, or what?"

Sandie stopped flicking through the magazine she'd just bought and tuned into our conversation instead.

"Very funny," I sighed, turning away from Kyra and tugging at the bottom of my huge (actually, *Dad*'s huge) jersey. "I'm feeling fat and this hides me, OK?"

Fat as an over-inflated lilo, if you want to know.

"Ally! You're *not* fat!" Sandie blinked at me in surprise.

"Sandie, my stomach's as bloated as your mum's," I whined, "but at least your mum's got an excuse, being five months' pregnant!"

"Lemme see this big, fat belly..." said Kyra, startling me by reaching over and hauling up both my jersey and my school shirt.

"Kyra!" I gasped, trying to yank my clothes back down.

"OK, so you're a bit squishy," she announced matter-of-factly, poking her finger in my tummy and making me squeak 'cause it tickled. "But it's not *too* bad."

"Gee, thanks..." I mumbled sarkily, tucking in my shirt again.

"And at least you can get rid of it. At least you don't have sticky-out ears like mine," said Kyra.

They weren't quite getting-stuck-in-a-lift-door material, but Kyra's ears definitely did stand to attention and face front.

"And at least you've got lovely thick hair, Ally," Sandie chipped in, twiddling a finger round her wispy, fair ponytail. "Mine is just *useless*!"

"Do you think boys stress out about stuff like this?" I asked my friends, as I deliberately stuck my tummy out just to see how horrendously huge I could make it look.

"Dunno," said Kyra, picking at the grass. "Whenever I've been out with a boy, it's not like I have that kind of conversation. I don't want to go moaning to a lad about the size of my ears or my bum or something, in case he notices and thinks, 'Oh yeah! She's right!', and dumps me!"

"OK, so you don't talk to *boyfriends* about what bits of yourself bug you," I shrugged, "but what about boy *mates*? Have you ever known a boy mate to whinge on about their bodies?"

"*What* boy mates?" Kyra frowned at me, as she picked bits of grass off her skirt. "I've only ever had boy*friends*."

Wow – and there was me, the total opposite. Zilch boyfriends (a couple of boring dates with Keith Brownlow in the dim, dark past doesn't count) and a lifelong buddy in the shape of Billy. Who moaned about a lot of things (never having snogged anyone, never been anywhere *near* snogging anyone, missing a goal at footie practice etc.), but never once moaned about his body. Well, only standard stuff about spots and how they always erupt whenever he's in sniffing distance of any girls he likes.

"You've never had a boy who's just a mate?" I quizzed Kyra.

That was a weird thought. Everyone I knew had boy mates. Look at me. Look at my sisters. Rowan had grunge-boy Chazza, and Linn had the wondrous, the gorgeous, the one-and-only Alfie (the one boy I definitely *wouldn't* want just as a mate – if you see what I mean).

"Course I haven't. They don't exist," Kyra said sniffily. "Girls and lads can never be proper friends. Fancying each other always gets in the way."

"That is *so* not true!" I argued. "Is it Sandie?"

But instead of backing me up, Sandie just bit her lip and shrugged.

"But come on, Sand!" I protested. "You've got boy mates! You've got ... er ... Billy!"

"Well, technically, he's *your* friend, not mine," Sandie said uneasily.

"See?" Kyra exclaimed triumphantly. "Even Sandie agrees with me!'

"Yeah?" I replied, widening my eyes and feeling horribly outnumbered. "Well, so much for your theory, Kyra. 'Cause me and Billy have known each other since nursery, and there's never been anything weird between us!"

(By weird, I meant lovey-dovey, but I just couldn't bring myself to say it out loud. The idea of me and Billy snogging or whatever ... *please*.)

11

"Poor Billy..." Kyra shrugged. "He's probably fancied you all this time and you've just never noticed..."

Arrrghh! She was *so* infuriating. But I knew she wasn't going to let me win this argument, so I did the only tactical thing I could think of.

I went in a huff.

Kyra was snickering behind me, but I kept silently staring off into the distance, acting like the top of the Telecom Tower, kilometres away in the distance, in the muddle of high-rise buildings in central London, was just about the most fascinating thing I'd ever seen.

"Aww. Are you in a huff with me?"

I ignored her. *And* Sandie, even though she wasn't saying anything.

"Not going to talk?"

Not in a million years, I said to myself silently. *Or at least till you apologize for winding me up, Kyra Davies...*

"Will you talk to me if I tell you about this brilliant new game I know?"

Nope, I muttered inside my head.

"It's fun ... it's a love game. Like a destiny thing. Who's the perfect boy for you sort of thing."

I didn't flinch. Even though it sounded interesting.

I couldn't resist those list games that me and all the other girls did. You know the sort: write down the names of the *five* cutest boys at school; write down the names of the *six* pop stars you'd most like to be stranded on a desert island with; write down the names of the *three* boys in class you'd like to kiss the *least*, and then name the one you'd snog if you absolutely *had* to. Yep, me and Chloe and Salma and everyone could waste hour after hour doing that stuff, no problem.

"Right then," said Kyra breezily. "Just me and Sandie will play then. All you need is six bits of paper and an empty crisp bag. I'm sure I've got one in here somewhere…"

As she rustled away in her black suede rucksack, temptation got the better of me. (Wow, my huff lasted for all of ten seconds. What amazing will power. Not.)

"OK, I'll play," I muttered. "How does it work?"

Kyra grinned at me, but didn't tease me any more. Thank goodness.

"Well," she began, now that she'd found an empty bag of Chipsticks and shaken the last crumbs out. "First we all have to write down six boys' names on little bits of paper—"

"In secret? Or do we show each other?" Sandie butted in excitedly.

"Um … in secret," Kyra replied hesitantly, which made me suspect she'd just made this game up.

Not that I cared. It still sounded fun.

"And then you scrunch up the names," Kyra continued, "and drop them all into the crisp bag. Then you close your eyes and pull one scrunched-up bit of paper out, and whoever's name is written on there – well, that's who you're destined to be with!"

As she talked, I'd already yanked my ring binder from my bag, flipped it to the back where there was plenty of blank paper, and started doodling down my six names. Carefully, I tore around each one, and crumpled the pieces up, till there was a small pile of paper balls on the grass in front of me.

"Sandie, you want to go first?" Kyra asked, holding the crinkling bag out towards her.

"Yeah, all right!" Sandie smiled, dropping her scraps of paper into it.

"Go on, then, pick one out!" Kyra ordered her, after shaking the bag about for *ages*. (I'd doodled some more names on the ripped back page of my ring binder – complete with swirly flowers and a few lovehearts – by the time she'd stopped mucking about.)

"Eeek!" squealed Sandie, pulling her hand out and unravelling her scrap of paper. "It's Brad Pitt!

14

I'm destined to be with Brad Pitt!"

Hmmm. Somehow I didn't think *that* was going to happen in a hurry.

"Sandie! You were meant to put in *real* people!" Kyra grumbled, emptying the rest of Sandie's choices on to the grass. "Here – take that!"

"Oh…" Sandie mumbled, grabbing the empty crisp bag and holding it out so Kyra could have her turn.

(By the way, see that scrap of paper with Brad's name on it? Sandie's still got it in this little jewelled box she keeps in her bedside drawer, like it'll bring her luck – or Brad – one day. Funnily enough, we haven't spotted him around Crouch End *yet*…)

"In they go!" said Kyra, kissing her closed hand first, before dropping the paper balls in the bag. "And the winner is…!"

I stopped doodling as she started un-scrunching, and waited with bated breath to see which poor boy Destiny had matched up Kyra with.

"Daniel Ade! Rats!" Kyra frowned.

"He's pretty cute!" I pointed out, wondering why she was moaning, when *she* was the one who'd written his name down.

"I know he's cute, but I wanted it to be Ricardo!"

I didn't see why. The only thing she and her boyfriend Richie/Ricardo seemed destined to do was keep splitting up every five minutes. I think they spend more time breaking up and making up than actually going out together properly.

"Come on – your turn, Ally!" said Kyra, sticking the bag under my nose.

"Uh – you want to empty it first?" I asked her.

Knowing that Richie/Ricardo was still lurking in there gave me the heeby-jeebies. There was no way I wanted to pull his name out and spend the rest of my life with a big-headed creep like him.

"Oops!" giggled Kyra, tipping out the bag, and then holding it out for me to inspect.

"OK," I nodded, chucking in my paper balls now that I could see that Richie/Ricardo wasn't lurking in either corner. "Wish me luck!"

"Luck!" Sandie smiled at me, knowing exactly whose name I wanted to pull out of that bag.

Kyra did her shaky-bag thing, then let me pick my destiny…

"It's…" I began, unfurling the salt-and-vinegar-scented scrap of paper. "It's … Alfie!"

"Oh, Ally!" gasped Sandie, clapping her hands together excitedly.

"Ooo-*oo*-ooh!" teased Kyra, arching her eyebrows at me. "Alfie and Ally, up a tree, K-I-S-S-I-N-G!"

"Shut up!" I laughed at her, while my cheeks went luminous pink with happiness.

"Oh, that's so brilliant, Ally!" Sandie gushed. "How lucky is that, to get Alfie's name? It was meant to be!"

I smiled shyly and shrugged, and couldn't quite look either of my friends in the eyes. Sandie was right, of course – it *was* meant to be. Only it didn't have much to do with luck.

Well, it couldn't really, could it? Not when I'd doodled Alfie's name on *all* six bits of paper...

Chapter 3

HOW TO BE A DORK,
BY ALLY LOVE, AGED THIRTEEN

Girls and boys can never be proper friends.

What a load of cobblers...

Honestly, Kyra Davies has a one-track mind! I thought to myself, as I ambled home from the park, twirling the piece of paper with Alfie's name on around in my fingers. *Just 'cause she only sees boys as potential snoggees, she thinks that goes for* everyone...

Well, she was wrong. I mean, half the world is filled with blokes, right? And you can't fancy them *all*, so that means there's plenty left over to be potential mates.

So, how do you tell the difference? How do you know which category (i.e. Fancying or Friendship) a lad fits into? Well here's my theory: if you can speak to a boy as easily as a girl, he's mate-material. But if you turn into a tongue-tied, bumbling geek with a brain of mush in front of a lad, then he's in the Fancying category.

And if there was one person guaranteed to

turn me into a bumbling, tongue-tied geek with a brain of mush, it was the person whose name was slithering through my fingers right now.

Alfie, Alfie, Alfie...

How many nights had I lain awake running his name through my mind?

Answer: more times than there are stars in the sky. Probably.

Ally, Ally, Ally...

How many nights had Alfie lain awake running my name through his mind?

Answer: never. Almost definitely.

Bummer.

Of course, apart from boys of the fancying or friendship variety, there's *another* category: the ones you're related to. As I got closer to the house, all thoughts of Alfie slipped from my mind as I tried to figure out what my little brother was up to. From my angle, I could just make out Tor in our tiny, overgrown front garden, peering at a removal van that was parked outside the house next door. Every couple of seconds, I could see Rolf's head too, as he bounced up and down to try and see whatever was holding his human buddy's attention.

"Gotcha!" I roared, after slipping silently through the gate (a miracle, with that squeaky old pile of wood and rusty hinges) and pouncing on my brother.

"Ally!" he yelped. "I – I *knew* it was you!"

It was only a white lie, and it was quite funny really, seeing how caught-in-the-act red-faced Tor was.

"What are you doing?" I asked, hunkering down and joining him and Rolf behind their hideaway hedging.

It was quite nice down there; like a secret world. Hidden under the bushes were clumps of yellow and white flowers, bravely struggling to grow in the shade, and a whole bunch of sparkly glass marbles that were half-buried at the root of the prickly bush I was avoiding getting too close to. For about half a second I wondered how those marbles came to be there, before realizing it was blindingly obvious. After all, who in our house was guilty of regularly nicking stuff and squirrelling it away? Yep, this secret stash had Winslet's pawmarks all over it...

"We're spying. New people!" said Tor, pointing towards the removal van.

It *was* quite exciting. It would be great if we got some friendly new neighbours, and you certainly couldn't describe the Fitzpatricks – who'd moved out the day before – as friendly, unless you started the word "friendly" with an "un" in front of it. Grumpy old Mr and Mrs Fitzpatrick had lived next door for *hundreds* of years, getting older and grumpier as time went by, and I don't think anyone living round here was exactly heartbroken to see them leave Palace Heights Road for their new sheltered home. I know that sounds really mean, but *you* try living next door to people who *growl* at you when you go past.

"So who're our new neighbours, then, Tor?" I asked my brother.

"Not them," Tor replied, pointing to two guys in matching red boiler suits staggering out of the lorry with a long, black leather sofa.

"Well, I think I can figure out for myself that the removal men aren't moving in!" I grumbled, prodding Tor in the stomach and making him giggle.

It was then – thanks to being crouched down – that I spotted the edge of something sticking out of his trouser pocket.

"What's this?" I asked, grabbing it, then stopping dead when I realized it was the last photo Mum had sent of herself – from Canada this time.

I'd wondered where it had gone – I'd spotted that it was missing from the pinboard in the kitchen last week.

"It's just Mum," Tor shrugged, grabbing the snap back.

Aw, bless. That made me go kind of *churny* inside, thinking of Tor taking that photo and carrying it around with him. It was *so* sweet (and so sad too). Well, whatever *I* was feeling *he* was looking embarrassed, so I decided to talk about the new neighbours again to give him a chance to stop blushing.

"So apart from the delivery men," I started chattering, "haven't you seen anyone else go in next door?"

"A big, tall man arrived," Tor whispered, shoving the picture back in his pocket. "He had an aquarium!"

Ah, so that was why Tor's radar was up. A fish fan moving in to No. 26 had his instant attention. I swear, a psychotic serial killer could move in next door, but if he had a hamster, Tor would immediately see him as a fellow pet-loving pal. I could tell straight away that I was going to have to restrain Tor from trotting up to the front door and trying to wangle an invite to inspect the New Neighbour's pets and swap tales of fin-rot.

"OK, so we know there's a big, tall man and some fish moving in," I said, slapping my hands on my bended knees. "But what about gorgeous teenage-boy love gods? Seen any of *them* carrying suitcases inside?"

I was only fooling around, and fooling around with Tor is fun – he's always guaranteed to snigger at even my most rubbish jokes. But my blood ran cold when I heard someone else – *two* someone elses – sniggering at what I'd just said.

"Yeah? *You* should be so lucky!" Linn teased me, pulling the front door closed behind her. "If a – what was it? – oh yeah, 'love god' did move in next door, he sure wouldn't be looking at *you*, Ally!"

I could have handled Linn taking the mickey out of me – hey, as my big sister, it was part of her job – but I couldn't bear the fact that Alfie was standing by her side, grinning down at me.

What impression must I have given him, hunkered down beside the bushes in my school skirt, looking like I was having a *wee* or something, and wittering on about "love gods"? OK, let's just say that the phrase running through his mind wasn't "Mmm – Linn's sister is *so* fanciable! How come I never noticed before?"

"C'mon, Alfie – let's leave the kids to play in the bushes!" Linn grinned wickedly, yanking the creaky gate open and heading out on to the pavement.

"Sarcasm is a really pathetic way to get laughs, and you're only showing off in front of Alfie!" I stood up and shouted after her.

All right, that's a lie. I didn't.

But I wish I had, instead of staying crouched down exactly where I was, wishing that just for once, I could look like a reasonable sane, attractive person in front of Alfie, instead of a complete *dork*.

"Oh, by the way," Linn's voice suddenly hovered somewhere above me, along with a rustle of leaves as she parted the foliage to stare down at me. "Your boyfriend Billy phoned for you about five minutes ago."

"He is *not* my boy –"

...friend, I was going to protest, but Linn and Alfie had already wandered off, lazily chatting to each other, before I'd got the chance to finish.

"That's *it*!" I spluttered to myself, stomping irritably towards the front door and leaving Tor and Rolf to their detective duties.

"It" was basically fancying boys. And "it" seemed to lead to nothing but humiliation. Turning into a tongue-tied, bumbling geek with a brain of mush ... getting caught drivelling on about "love-gods" in front of Alfie ... it was more than my fragile self-confidence could stand. There was only one thing I could do – from now on I was going to harden my heart towards Alfie (and any other random, second-division crushes I sometimes indulged in) and stick to boys as friends *only*. It was a lot less traumatic.

And anyway, apart from the humiliation, what boy could fancy me with my fat little jelly belly?

"Billy?" I bleated down the phone, desperate to hear a male voice that wasn't sniggering at my stupidness.

"Nyuh? Hewow? Aaawwwy?"

Luckily, I knew this language Billy was suddenly talking. Let me interpret: "Nyuh? Hewow? Aaawwwy?" translates as "Yeah? Hello? Ally?" The root of this ancient language is English, which is then mixed with a gob full of peanut-butter sandwich. It has no official name, but I like to call it "Pigface".

"Yeuchh!" I winced, holding the receiver away from my ear. "Billy, *don't* eat while you're on the phone to someone! It's totally disgusting!"

"Ung, sowwwy. Hoe on…"

(Translation: "Oh, sorry, hold on … I'm a total dweeb and don't deserve to have a friend as pretty and talented as you." OK – so I might have made the last bit up.)

It sounded like Billy had stepped away from the phone, hopefully to finish chewing however much sandwich he still had rammed in his mouth.

"Hi! How're you doing!" Billy said breezily after half a nano-second, which was a suspiciously short time for him to have chomped and swallowed. I had this horrible vision of him spitting half a mangled mouthful of bread and peanut butter into his hand so he could continue our conversation.

Bleurghhh…

"I'm all right," I shrugged, even though he couldn't see me hunch my shoulders. "So what's going on?"

Normally when I ask him that, he'll say "Nothin'", or, if he's having a *really* wild day, "Not much".

But today – well, knock me down with a very large feather – something was going on. A *couple* of somethings, as I found out.

"Listen," he said, lowering his voice, "Mum and Dad are going out to a party tomorrow night, and I was thinking of getting a few mates around."

"Yeah?" I replied, perking up. "Like who?"

"Well, like Steven and Hassan and Richie. And you, of course. And your mates."

"What? All of them? Like Chloe and Jen and everyone?"

"No, not all of them," he hissed down the phone, obviously trying to keep the Saturday night mate-fest quiet from his folks. "Just maybe Sandie. And Kyra, course, since Richie's coming."

Hmm. Could be a laugh. Billy's school buddies Steven and Hassan were all right. Not cute or fanciable, I mean, but pretty funny sometimes. Yep – tomorrow could be kind of cool. A definite improvement on staying in and slagging off all the contestants on *The X-Factor*, that was for sure.

"Right – I'll phone Sandie and Kyra and see if they fancy it," I replied, tangling the phone cord round in my fingers.

"Brilliant!" Billy responded, a bit too loud. Quick as a flash, he dropped his voice again. "Listen, if you bump in to my mum tomorrow during the day at the shops or anything, don't let on, yeah?"

As if I would. Billy's mum was really house-proud and pernickety (put a cup down on the table without a coaster and consider yourself never invited round again), and the idea of Billy having a noisy, potentially messy bunch of mates round without her there to oversee the proceedings (with a pair of rubber gloves on and a can of Pledge in her hand) was unthinkable.

"Sure," I nodded to the lavender-coloured hallway wall. "So what time should we come round?"

"About half-seven. Oh, and Ally – there's something else," he whispered so low that I had to press the phone right up to my ear.

"What?" I quizzed him, finding myself whisper-ing too – who knows why, since the only pair of ears listening in to my end of the conversation belonged to a cat that wasn't Colin, who was gently snorey-purring through the bannisters behind me on the stairs.

"Can't tell you now – someone might be listening. Tell you when I see you tomorrow night."

"Aw, come on – that's not fair! You've got to give me a little clue at least!" I teased him. "Just whisper it!"

Hurrah – my whining worked. He gave me a clue all right – a great, big, fat one.

"OK," he hissed, sounding strangely wobbly. "It's just that I think … I think I'm in love!"

Billy in love? For real? For *real* real? Not just fancying someone?

Well, blow me down with a whole *bunch* of feathers. This was serious. And weird. Actually, hearing his news right there? That's how I felt – seriously weird…

Chapter 4

THE AMAZING HUMAN CAT CUSHION...

One day later, detective Tor was still on duty, and no closer to solving the mystery of who the new neighbours were.

"Isn't he bored yet?" mumbled Rowan, as Tor zoomed back out into the garden, after his latest "Still no sign of anyone!" bulletin.

Whoever had moved in was probably hiding behind the curtains and looking up the number of the local police station so they could report the mini-stalker they'd spotted spying on them.

"Mmm," I muttered in reply, lying stretched out on the sofa and staring at Saturday-morning TV with Colin curled up on my comfy cushion of a stomach. (I was glad someone liked it, since I certainly didn't.)

"Did he go on about it when you two went up to the pet shop?" Rowan asked, swivelling her breakfast (a strawberry-flavoured lollipop) from one side of her mouth to the other.

"Yep," I nodded, still staring past Colin's

twitching ginger ears at the telly.

Tor had wittered on about the Fish Fan next door all the way up to the Broadway and back on our regular weekly pet-supplies forage. Well, as much as Tor *can* witter. As anyone who knows him knows, he doesn't *do* long sentences, just shrugs, looks and short sound bites. But he sure was stringing a lot of sound bites together in an excited sort of way when it came to our new neighbours.

(Rolf seemed to be less than excited, though – he'd given up acting the police dog, and instead of bounding in and out of the garden alongside Tor, he was now trying to fold his long, floppy body around my feet at the other end of our squashy sofa.)

For a few minutes there was silence, as Rowan, Colin, Rolf and I tuned into the TV, listening to the two presenters jabbering away, acting like hyper nine year olds, even though they were dressed as if they were ready to go out to a club any second.

"See those two?" Rowan suddenly came out with, wafting her lollipop towards the blonde girl and the spiky-haired guy on the screen. "I'm *sure* they fancy each other."

"How do you figure that one out?" I turned to frown at Rowan, and instantly wished I hadn't.

Curled up on one of the armchairs, she was a bundle of so many colours and patterns, it was enough to give you a migraine – and she hadn't even got dressed yet. I tried to take in the turquoise scrunchie tying up her bed-head hair, her black, orange and yellow silky floral kimono, her red and green tartan pyjamas and her bright pink furry piggy slippers and immediately narrowed my eyes against the glare. Focusing on Rowan right then was a bit like staring into a kaleidoscope when you're feeling travel-sick.

"Well, *look* at the two of them!" said Rowan vehemently. "They're *always* flirting with each other!"

"They *work* together! They're just good friends!" I blurted out in the presenters' defence, squinting at Rowan till my eyes got over the shock. "Why do people have to assume a boy and a girl fancy each other just 'cause they get on well?"

"I was only *saying*!" Rowan shrugged back at me. "Why are you so jumpy about it?"

Why *was* I so jumpy? I wondered, surprised at myself for overreacting.

Part of me instantly thought about what Billy had told me in the phone last night, about being "in love", but as quickly as I'd thought about that, I chucked it out of my mind. Of *course* that couldn't have anything to do with why I was jumpy. Then I remembered sitting up on the slope beside Ally Pally the previous afternoon, listening to Kyra's dumb opinions about being friends with boys and how you *couldn't* be. Not to mention getting creeped out at the very idea of anything squelchy and smoochy – yuck! – going on between me and Billy *ever*. Yep – *that* must be what was preying on my mind.

"Aw, it was just that Kyra wound me up yesterday," I explained. "She's got this stupid theory..."

"Yeah? What about?"

"Well, *she* says girls and lads can never really be friends, 'cause fancying each other always gets in the way. But that's not right, is it? You don't think that's true, do you, Ro? I mean, you and Chazza..."

Rowan giggled so much she had to take the lollipop out of her mouth, to make sure she didn't *choke*.

"Me and *Chazza*? God, *no*! I could *never* fancy him! He's my mate!" she grinned, sounding half-amused, half-horrified at the very idea.

"Well, that's what I mean," I replied, trying to wriggle to a more upright position, without disturbing Colin or Rolf. "It's like Kyra thinks boys and girls are a different species or something, and that's *so* not true – we're all the same!"

"Apart from the fact that we've got bumps in different places!" Rowan snickered, narrowing her eyes wickedly at me.

"You *know* what I mean," I said snippily, feeling myself do the flush-blush.

"Yeah, well I agree with you, *kind* of," Rowan continued, swivelling round in her seat and dangling her skinny legs and her fat furry piggy slippers over the arm of the chair. "But there are big differences between the way boys and girls *think*."

"Like how?" I asked her.

This was pretty interesting. Rowan might act like such a ditzy airhead sometimes that I feel like I'm *her* big sister, but when it comes to hanging out with older people, she's definitely got the edge on me. Maybe she could give me some insights – stuff that I could use the *next* time Kyra started spouting her made-up theories of boys versus girls.

"Well, it's kind of corny to say," she began, "but girls are definitely better at showing their emotions than boys."

I immediately got a vision of the last movie me, Sandie and Billy went to see. As the hero lay dying in the heroine's arms – covered in blood and guts and stuff – Sandie was sobbing (so loud I thought we'd get chucked out), *I* had a lump as hard as a walnut in my throat (not to mention a seriously quivery lip), but when I looked around at Billy, all *he* was doing was picking his nose and yawning.

Maybe Rowan had a point about the emotions thing.

"And boys can't help acting tough in front of other lads," Rowan continued. "It's like Chazza – did I tell you he's got a band together at college?"

"Yeah," I shrugged casually. "You said something about that."

Huh – how could I forget? The minute she'd told me I had visions of Chazza turning up on *MTV* and me squealing "I *know* him! I *know* him!" to Chloe and Kellie and everyone.

"Well, he's started hanging out with the guys in the band more, instead of me and Von, like it's not *cool* to have girls as best mates any more."

Especially Rowan, I thought. What would eighteen- or nineteen-year-old lads make of Chazza having a best mate who's a fifteen-year-old schoolgirl?

Well, at least it made me realize I could always rely on Billy, even if he *did* eat peanut-butter sandwiches in my ear down the phone.

"I saw white fur!" Tor interrupted us, coming crashing into the living room and rudely waking up the snoozing pets.

"Where?" asked Rowan.

"At the patio doors!"

Me and Rowan looked at each other. Our house didn't *have* patio doors – the closest we got to one of those was a small paw-mark-smeared cat flap cut in the bottom of the back door.

"Maybe – maybe it's a West Highland terrier!" said Tor breathlessly. "*They're* white!"

"Tor! You haven't been climbing over the garden wall, have you?" I asked him, realizing that he *had* to be talking about next-*door*'s patio.

How embarrassing. The new neighbours would think we hadn't had him house-trained yet.

"No!" he protested. "I've been standing on the swing, going really high, so I can see over the wall!"

And with that he was off again, for more swinging and spying.

"He'll be begging us to get the trampoline out next," Rowan grinned, rolling her eyes.

Our old mini-trampoline, all dusty and dis-mantled, was stored in the loft cupboard between my attic bedroom and Linn's. I'd forgotten all about it.

"Maybe *I* need to get the trampoline out," I sighed, pointing towards my stomach, "to get rid of *this*!"

"What – Colin?" Rowan frowned, staring over at the snoozly cat.

"No! My flabby tummy!"

"Ally, you have *not* got a flabby tummy!" said Rowan adamantly.

"How do *you* know?" I argued. "*You're* not the one that has to look at it *wobbling* in the bath!"

"Well, everyone gets a bit wobbly sometimes!" she persisted. "All you do is cut out chocolate and stuff and it'll go away!"

"But that's why it's not fair!" I whined. "I don't even eat much sweet stuff!"

"OK, but the crisps and Coke you like aren't exactly calorie-free."

Drat.

Double drat.

She'd got me right where it hurt.

I mean, maybe I could swap to Diet Coke or something, but with me and nachos, it was practically a *love* affair. How could I give them up?

"Why don't you just try and do a bit more exercise?" Rowan suggested.

Mmm ... if I did more exercise, could I lose the pudgy tum and *still* get away with eating vats of kettle crisps 'n' dips?

"But what kind of exercise is good for flabby stomachs?" I asked her, putting my hands on either side of my tummy and wobbling it, making

Colin spread out all three of his legs to keep his balance.

"Well, probably a proper keep-fit class. Aerobics or something."

I think Rowan must have seen the fear in my face. I'd peeked into the exercise classes when I was passing the YMCA before, and no *way* could little old me walk into a class of those grown-up scary women in their Lycra thongs.

"Look, Von's big sister is into stuff like that. I'll ask her what classes are in this area, and ... and I'll come along with you, if you want."

I was still pretty frazzled at the idea of going to a proper class, but if Rowan was up for coming too, it could possibly, *maybe* be OK.

"Don't get too used to that, Colin," I said to His Gingerness, as he padded about on my tummy, getting comfy again. "'Cause it's not going to stay!"

Yep, Operation Jelly Belly had begun...

Chapter 5

SATURDAY NIGHT NIGHTMARE

Kyra was wrong, I was right.

Billy was as good a mate to me as any of my girlfriends. And I was going to point that out to Kyra tonight, when we all hung out together. Well, that was the plan, till Billy and his stupid boy-buddies trashed my theory…

The time: 9 p.m. Saturday night.

The place: Billy's living room.

The people: on the girls' team – me, Kyra and Sandie. On the boys' team – Billy (natch), Richie/Ricardo (unfortunately), Steven Briggs (lanky, smiley, a bit join-the-dots spotty) and Hassan Khan (small, wiry, cute in a gerbily kind of way). Oh, and Precious (small, annoying, poodle).

Fun factor: a big fat zero and falling.

In fact right at that moment, me, Sandie and Kyra were sitting together on the sofa *wincing*.

How come?

Well, Billy's mate Steven had just leapt on to the coffee table, launched into the chorus of this awful football chant thing, only to be immediately jumped on by a roaring Billy, Richie and Hassan, who did some kind of rugby tackle on him that hurled Steven off the table and splatted him right in the middle of the living-room floor. We had absolutely no idea why. (And I don't think the boys really did either.)

The three of us girls had been at Billy's for over an hour, and it was getting less fun by the second.

The Saturday night festivities had started out medium-to-boring, with the boys doing lots of shuffling about and sniggering when we arrived, as if they'd never *seen* girls before. And it had started the second Sandie, Kyra and I had stepped through the front door, right after Precious had tried to burst our eardrums with his yapping.

"Hi, Ricardo!" Kyra had grinned, walking towards her boyfriend in the hall and aiming a hello kiss at him.

She was expecting maybe a hug or a kiss back. She *wasn't* expecting him to snort "*Pwwwahhhh!*" very loudly and run away from her giggling, hiding behind the other lads from her as if she was a *flu* germ or something.

"Why is Ricardo being like that to you?" Sandie frowned, totally confused.

"Showing off in front of his mates," Kyra sighed,

39

folding her arms across her chest, and watching her boyfriend scamper off with his friends like some demented puppy.

And so for most of the hour we'd been there, all four boys spent their time ignoring us and playing *Return of the Donkey Tomb Raiders Speed Death Race* or whatever on Billy's PlayStation.

And they wouldn't let any of us have a turn.

OK, so sitting talking to my two mates on a sofa is all very nice, but we could have done that somewhere else, without being drowned out by boys roaring "Oi!", "Gimme!", "S'my turn!", "No way!" and "Bog off!" very loudly in the background.

At one point, I knew things were *really* going to go downhill when I asked Hassan to put on another CD. Maybe I'm just being stupid or something, but I thought this was a pretty straightforward suggestion, considering that a) the last CD had just finished, and b) Hassan was sitting right next to the midi-system and the pile of CDs Billy had brought down from his room. But oh, no.

"Put on another CD! Put on another CD!" Hassan repeated in a tiny, high-pitched squeal, which I think was meant to be *me*. It was pathetic. It didn't sound anything like me, and what I'd said wasn't weird or stupid enough to take the mickey out of. So why did Hassan and all three of the

other lads descend into fits of sniggen.

And now they were showing off in fro.
piling on top of Steven and doing that ro.
thing. I mean *roaring*, for goodness' sake. What .
all that about? Could some boy please take time
out to come and tell me why guys have to *roar*
when they get together?

The roaring. The going-all-shy in the company
of girls but still-showing-off stuff. There could
only be one reason for all this drongo behaviour.

"Oi!" I yelled over at the lads.

Amongst the scrum of flailing arms and legs and
a growling dog, four grinning red faces turned and
looked questioningly at me.

"Do you lot like burgers?" I asked, gazing at
each sweaty face in turn.

"Yeah!" they all replied enthusiastically.

I think maybe they thought I was about to offer
to go and *make* some or something.

Fat chance…

"Do you eat a *lot* of burgers?" I quizzed the lads
again.

"S'pose so," grunted Richie/Ricardo, while the
other three just nodded.

"There you go," I exclaimed, ignoring the boys
now and turning back to my two sane girlfriends.

"What?" Sandie asked.

"BSE. That Mad Cow Disease. Remember that? They've all got it. It's the only explanation," I shrugged.

"Not true!" Billy roared, before Steven got him in a head-lock and thundered him down towards the carpet.

"You two got any money?" Kyra yawned, taking no notice at all of the boys and their roaring bundle.

"Some. Why?" I asked, sticking my hand in the back pocket of my trousers to make sure I'd definitely brought my tenner allowance money with me, and not left it sitting on the kitchen table at home. (A dangerous thing to do – not because my sisters or Tor might go off with it, but because Winslet might be tempted to nick it for her latest stash of Precious Things.)

"Well, I was thinking we could go to that really good pizza place up in Muswell Hill," Kyra suggested, checking her nails as she addressed me and Sandie.

"Oh, yeah! La Porchetta, you mean?" said Sandie, brightening up. "It's not a long walk from here and they always play really fun music in there!"

"Hey, hey, Ally!" Billy protested, wriggling free from his head-lock now that he'd cottoned on to the escape plan us girls were hatching. "You lot can't go! We're having fun!"

Me, Kyra and Sandie said absolutely nothing – we just stared at him long and hard.

He got the message.

"Hold on!" he announced, sounding a bit desperate if you ask me. "Got something really good! Me and the lads – we'll show you! Stay there! Don't move!"

"What? What are we supposed to be doing?" asked Richie/Ricardo, narrowing his eyes at Billy.

"Never mind! Just come on! Come with me, you guys!" Billy exclaimed, heading out of the living-room door and waving for the other three boys to follow him.

Blinking like babies that had just woken up, Richie/Ricardo, Steven and Hassan lolloped after him, followed by a four-legged white ball of fuzz.

"Five minutes! Stay there!" Billy announced, reappearing at the living-room door with a stupid grin on his face, and motioning for me and the girls to stay put.

"What are you lot up to?" I asked him, but he'd already disappeared again, thundering upstairs with his buddies.

"What's all that about?" Kyra queried, sprawling herself back on the sofa and staring at the ceiling above us, where we could hear lots of thumping feet, more yapping, more giggling and yet *more* roaring.

"Don't ask me," I mumbled, already daydreaming about which pizza to have at La Porchetta.

"Billy's mum's really fussy, isn't she?" Sandie suddenly happened to mention.

"Yeah – why?" I replied.

Billy's house looked like a bunch of pages torn out of an IKEA catalogue, it was so pristine and perfect. Well, at least it was normally.

"She's going to flip when she sees this, then!" said Sandie, glancing nervously around the room.

She was right. A small platoon of soldiers ransacking the place would have made less mess. And the mess – crisps scrunched into the carpet, empty drinks cans, cushions all over the floor, CDs and CD covers tossed all over the place, size forty trainer footprints smeared on to the glass of the coffee table – was most definitely boy-based. Us three girls had done nothing but sit on the sofa and sip on the same cans of Coke we'd had when we first got there (mainly because the boys had drunk everything else in the fridge before we arrived).

"It'll be OK," I suggested, dubiously. "Billy's parents aren't getting back from their party till after midnight. He'll have plenty of time to tidy up."

Who was I kidding? It would be obvious to anyone who's ever peeked in his room. (don't bother – it's not a pretty sight) that Billy wasn't born with the tidiness gene.

"Stick the TV on, Ally," Kyra sighed, curling her long, skinny legs up under her. "Might as well have *some* entertainment tonight."

And so – once I'd found the melted-chocolate-covered remote – we whiled away ten minutes or so squinting at some quiz show thing through a haze of greasy fingerprints on the screen. Not that I was concentrating – I was too busy being annoyed with Billy for acting like a baboon, and ruining my chances of showing him off to Kyra as living proof of how fabulous a male mate could be. Meanwhile, there was still assorted whooping, thumping, laughing and barking going on upstairs.

And another thing, Billy might have promised to tell me more about this girl he was supposed to be in love with tonight, but it didn't exactly look like that was going to happen – not the way *he* was charging about with his hyperactive mates.

"He fancies you," said Kyra suddenly, her eyes still glued to the telly.

"Who fancies who?" asked Sandie, wide-eyed.

"Billy – he definitely fancies Ally," Kyra replied matter-of-factly.

"Kyra!" I gasped. "He does *not* fancy me! Where did you get that from?!"

"The way he's showing off. And the way he got all upset when he thought you were leaving…"

Kyra shot a cheeky, smirky look my way, just to check that she was winding me up properly. And she was.

"Kyra, they're *all* showing off! And he didn't want *any* of us to leave!" I spluttered.

"Nah – it's different when it comes to you," Kyra shook her head infuriatingly. "It's the way he looks at you, all sort of *longingly*…"

I knew (I hoped) she was only taking the mick (because she was bored), but that didn't stop the top of my head feeling like it was going to *explode*, I was so mad at her.

"Kyra—"

"Uh-oh – here they come," Sandie shushed us, hearing the clumping of feet hammering down the stairs. "Better get ready for their surprise!"

"Ooh, I can hardly wait!" said Kyra sarcastically, rolling her eyes roof-wards.

Sandie, meanwhile, just took a sip of her drink – and nearly choked on it when the lads burst through the door.

"*Whaaa!*" roared Billy, throwing his arms out wide, while the other boys struck stupid poses. "What do you think?"

I thought a few things. I thought…

1) What exactly were they supposed to be?

2) Had Billy gone mental?

3) Were we actually supposed to be entertained by this?

4) Who'd have guessed Billy's mum had such sexy underwear?

Not that it was sexy right now. All that slinky satin and lace looked about as saucy as a dead haddock, but then I guess it wasn't supposed to be worn by thirteen-year-old boys, especially over the top of their combat trousers and football shirts.

"What *do* you look like?" Kyra snarled at them.

"The Pussycat Dolls!" yelped Hassan. "Look! I'm Vanessa!"

He tried to do a karate-style move, only he hadn't pulled the red, slinky knickers up far enough, so instead of a high kick, there was just a loud rip.

"Hey, I thought we were supposed to be The Saturdays!?" frowned Steven.

"The Saturdays?!" snorted Kyra. "You're more like the *Tweenies*!"

But the boys hadn't heard – they were too busy arguing about which girl band they were meant to be. But to be honest, I don't think either the Pussycat Dolls or The Saturdays had ever worn a bra as a bandanna, like Billy was doing.

"How could you be Vanessa anyway, Hassan?" said Richie/Ricardo (in a purple bra-and-knicker combo). "You'd have to be Nicole!"

"But it's The Saturdays! So Hassan has to be Rochelle!" Steven yelped.

"Why do I have to be Nicole or Rochelle?" bellowed Hassan. "I'm not black, you muppet! My family's from Pakistan!"

"Whatever! Who cares?" grinned Richie/Ricardo cheekily, before pain got the better of him.

That was one mighty bra-strap *ping!* Hassan gave him. That would *definitely* leave a bruise...

Who knows how long the boys would have spent arguing and happily winding each other up in women's underwear? Hours probably, only me and the girls wouldn't have been around to see it (a pepperoni pizza at La Porchetta was looking more enticing by the second). But the fooling around only lasted about three seconds more, since the rightful owner of the knickers walked in right at that moment.

And by the look on her face, it seemed like Billy's mum really, *really* didn't think his lace-edged home-boy bandanna suited him too much...

Chapter 6

THE BIRDS AND THE BEES (AND THE MICE...)

It was Sunday morning, and I was pooped, thanks to a nightmare.

It's not what you think – I wasn't dreaming about the horror of watching Baby Spice turning into Billy and proclaiming he loved me or anything (yuck). In fact, it wasn't even me who was doing the dreaming. Or the nightmaring. It was Tor – who came creeping (make that *thudding*) into my bed in the middle of the night, after bad dreams had woken him up. I squished over to make room for him, and hoped he'd drift off OK, but he ended up sinking into *Nightmare 2: The Sequel*, and kept muttering stuff I couldn't quite make out, although I did think he called out "Mum!" once, but I couldn't be sure, in amongst all the mumbo-jumbo mumblings. Incomprehensible or not, he was still being far more talkative than he ever is in the daytime, and I had to keep stroking his head or nudging him just to get him to shut up.

I felt like I lay awake in the dark for hours, while

Tor dream-babbled on, but I must have fallen asleep at some point – and when I finally woke up this morning, Mr Chatterbox was nowhere to be seen.

Yawning and still half-asleep, I took cat-steps down the stairs towards the kitchen and a big mug of tea to wake me up.

(Definition of cat-steps: two normal steps downstairs, followed by one big one, over the top of random snoozling furrballs dotted over the stairs.)

But I was soon to find that this was no ordinary Sunday morning – oh no. It turned out that there had been a Happy Event in our household – one of Tor's white mice had magically multiplied overnight, meaning that we had six new pink mini-mouse-mouths to feed.

"Isn't it great?" Tor turned round in his chair and beamed at me, none the worse for his nightmare, I noticed.

"Um…" I muttered, trying to read Dad's expression on the other side of the big kitchen table.

From the fleeting face he pulled at me, I felt that I might have walked in on a delicate situation.

"Of course it's great," Dad agreed with Tor, while scratching his head. "Only, like I was saying,

Tor, there might be even *more* babies to come, and then it's not such a good thing because how will we find homes for them all?"

As Dad spoke, I wandered over to the kettle and was sleepily pleased to see it had just been boiled.

"Anyone else want one?" I asked, plopping a tea bag into one of Mum's hand-made mugs. (Probably not a good choice for first thing in the morning – all the mugs Mum made have these wonky rims, and if you don't concentrate, tea often ends up slopping down your front as well as into your mouth.)

"No – I just got one," Dad answered, looking oddly nervous.

What was happening exactly? I wondered, gazing at my dad, in his jeans, ancient black T-shirt and sticking-up morning hair. Tor – sitting hugging an orange juice in his hands while still dressed in his Spiderman jim-jams – was staring at Dad questioningly.

"Why would there be more mice babies?" I asked, pulling out a chair and joining the boys.

As soon as I'd asked that, my just-coming-to-life-brain came up with another relevant question.

"How did *these* mice babies arrive? I thought you kept your boy and girl mice in separate cages?" I asked Tor.

"I let them play..." Tor mumbled in reply,

knowing now that this somehow *wasn't* the right thing to have done, even if he was a bit hazy on *why* exactly.

"He felt sorry for them, being kept apart," Dad explained to me, widening his brown eyes so I got the message.

"Ahhh…" I sighed, nodding at Dad. "And they ended up playing Mummies and Daddies?"

"Exactly," Dad nodded back at me. "And now Tor and me are just having a little chat. About the birds and the bees."

"And the mice," I added, with a grin, as I got up from the table.

"Uh … you don't have to go, Ally Pally!" said Dad, noticing that I was off-ski. "Maybe you could help explain … things."

Er – no thanks. The "Where Babies Come From" talk was definitely in the *Parents Handbook of Yukky Things To Do*, and I was not about to let Dad off the hook. Mum was the one who'd explained all that stuff to Linn and Rowan, but by the time I was asking awkward questions, Mum was gone, and it was Grandma who'd sat me down and filled me in on everything I needed to know. So now it was only fair that Dad took his turn, and had a serious man-to-boy chat.

"You'll be better at that sort of stuff on your

own, Dad," I said, scooting out of the kitchen as fast as I could and making a dash for the safety of the living room.

It was nice – there was no sign of Linn or Rowan yet so I had the big sunshine-yellow room all to myself, if you don't count Winslet rustling about, trying to get comfy on the beanbag.

I flicked on the TV, and flopped back on to the cushion-covered sofa. Last night's newspaper – lying scrunched and read at the end of the sofa – unexpectedly rustled into life.

"Prrrp!"

"Hello, Colin!" I cooed, as a ginger nose peeked out from under the printed pages.

Emerging from his hidey-hole, Colin did a long, slightly wobbly cat-stretch (that's three legs for you – you can't help the odd wobble), walked up the length of my legs and then started padding away with his paws on his new favourite place: my cushion of a tummy. Urgh – I'd completely forgotten about the jelly belly.

"Hi!" came Rowan's whispered voice, as she padded silently into the living room to join me. "Have you heard what's going on in the kitchen?"

Rowan, her hair a mass of frizzy, springy curls from some mad hairdo or other the night before, was grinning like crazy.

"What? Dad doing his big, parental talk?" I grinned back at her. "Didn't you fancy going in there and helping to bail him out?"

"No way!" giggled Rowan, sinking down on her knees beside the beanbag and giving Winslet's ears a scratch.

"Here," I muttered, stretching down for the wonky mug on the floor by the sofa. "Have some of my tea, since the kitchen's a no-go area."

"Thanks," she nodded, talking it from me. "So … what did you get up to last night, Ally Pally?"

"Not much. Just hung out at Billy's," I answered her, wincing inside at the memory of the rubbish Kyra had been coming out with and not wanting to go there again.

Then another memory from last night made me wince – the vision of Billy's mum's face in the living-room doorway…

Oh boy, Billy and the other lads had really got it. Which I can understand. I mean, poor Mrs Stevenson – the shame of walking into her house and seeing a bunch of lads prancing around in the contents of her underwear drawer… I think the migraine that had made her leave the party where she and Billy's dad had been had suddenly got a whole lot worse.

Luckily, I think it was blindingly obvious to Mr

and Mrs Stevenson that us girls were blameless in all this, and not *just* because none of us were wearing Mrs Stevenson's pants on our heads or anything. I think the fact that Kyra, Sandie and I had been sitting with our arms across our chests when they walked in, looking deeply unimpressed and unamused by our dorky male mates, showed straight away that we had in no way encouraged them in their rubbish girl-band impersonations. And just as well – since *my* dad went line-dancing (oh, the shame!) with Billy's parents every Wednesday night, and I didn't really want any bad reports of my behaviour getting back to him.

"Oh, hey!" said Rowan, after taking a couple of slurps of tea. "I almost forgot! Von's seen an ad on her college noticeboard for a class we can go to!"

"Yeah?" I blinked at her, feeling very awake and intrigued all of a sudden.

"And it's in a church hall not far from here, which is brilliant – in that modern red-brick church – what's it called again?" Rowan burbled.

"I dunno," I frowned at her, wishing she'd get to the point. "Anyway, what is—"

"And it's great, 'cause Von says she'll come too!"

I was still a bit confused about what exactly Rowan was on about, but I was quite chuffed at the idea of going to whatever class we were going to with Von in tow. I mean, my sister's friend was very cool, and the idea of little old me hanging out with her was … well, very cool.

"Isn't it exciting?" Rowan flashed her eyes wide at me.

"Well, yes, but—"

"It's on Tuesday night, at seven o'clock. Von says she'll get the phone number off the poster at college and find out what we need to wear and everything."

Wear? Didn't you just wear trackie bottoms and T-shirts and stuff to exercise classes?

"Ro?"

"What?" she smiled happily at me.

"What kind of class is it?"

"Didn't I say?" she frowned.

"Nope."

"Well, it's belly dancing, of course!"

"*Belly* dancing?!"

What was "of course" about *belly* dancing?

It was two days to go before I even stepped through the church-hall door and *already* I was feeling sick with nerves…

Chapter 7

BILLY AND THE BIG FAVOUR

"I *think* she'll forgive me," Billy shrugged, pulling the peak of his baseball cap down, as if he was in hiding from anyone in the park who might have heard about the underwear episode.

Not that anyone strolling about Alexandra Palace or its park was taking a blind bit of notice of two teenagers sitting on a bench this windy Sunday morning.

"Oh, yeah? And exactly *how* long do you think it'll take your mum to forgive you?" I said, keeping my gaze fixed on the three dogs whirling madly around us. Weirdly, I was feeling kind of shy in front of Billy this morning. Which wasn't weird at all – it was stupid, and it was all Kyra's fault. If I didn't keep remembering what she'd said last night, about Billy "fancying" me, I'd be OK. I'd have to kill Kyra next time I saw her...

"I don't think it'll take Mum *that* long to forgive me," Billy shrugged again. "Sometime in the next decade, hopefully. I mean, by the time I'm thirty-five, I'm sure she'll see the funny side…"

I giggled, and suddenly didn't feel shy of Billy any more. The thing is, Billy might be a berk, but he does make me smile sometimes. And I needed something to make me smile after Rowan terrifying me earlier with the news that we were going to a *belly*-dancing class.

"Well, forget your mum – haven't you got something else to tell me about?" I asked, sneaking a sideways peek at him. "Something you never got round to telling me about last night?"

See? This is what I should have said to Kyra last night – of *course* Billy didn't fancy me – he was in love with some girl or other, and he was going to tell me about it right now.

"Ah, The Girl!" he murmured wistfully, lifting his eyes to the fluffy-cloud-filled sky. "Wow, is she cute! She's seriously, seriously gorgeous!"

"Yeah, you said that much on the phone on Friday, but you promised me you'd tell me more about her last night," I pointed out. "And you didn't say one solitary thing."

"Um, I know," he grimaced, looking pinkly embarrassed, "but it all got a bit mad, with everyone round the house and everything."

"You mean you didn't want to talk about soppy

stuff like fancying this girl in front of your stupid laddish mates!" I teased him.

OK, this felt better, this felt normal. This was just mates talking.

"Something like that..." he grinned sheepishly.

"God, why do boys always have to have this big front when they're around other guys?" I sighed.

"Dunno," he said uselessly, shaking his head and staring down at the grass, where the green-ness was interspersed with furry blurs of scampering dogs.

"So come on – tell me all about this goddess!"

What number would this particular girl be? I tried to work out. Number 3,409 in Billy's long list of pointless crushes? All pointless, 'cause he never got beyond drooling from a distance.

"Well," Billy began, "she's got this sort of cropped black hair..."

"Uh-huh."

"...and these really nice freckles on her nose..."

"Uh-huh."

"...and a brilliant figure..."

"Uh-huh."

"And when she smiles..."

"Yeah, yeah, I get the message. She's gorgeous. But what about hard facts?" I hurried him along. "Where have you seen her? Who is she?"

You know, it was pretty odd, but all of a sudden, I was feeling a bit tetchy. Somehow, I just couldn't bear sitting here listening to him talk about how drop-dead fantastic someone's freckles were. Maybe it was just because I was in a bad mood about my jelly belly and wasn't particularly up for hearing about someone who obviously didn't have one.

"Um, well, she works up at that sports shop on Muswell Hill Broadway," he told me. "She works there Saturdays, and Thursdays after school."

"How do you know that?"

"'Cause when I was in there last Saturday – when I first saw her – I overheard her boss saying he'd see her on Thursday. And then I went in on Thursday night, and there she was, talking to another sales assistant about what had happened to her at school that day."

"So you just hung around the shop, listening in?" I asked, imagining him studying golf shoes or tennis skirts or something and pretending to be totally *fascinated* by them.

"No, I bought a pair of sports socks, just so I didn't look suspicious," he explained. "And then I bought another pair yesterday afternoon, when I went in to see her again..."

Uh-oh – Billy was stalking this girl from behind the sports-sock section. How sad was that?

"So, she's got to be at least fourteen to have a part-time shop job like that, doesn't she?" I pointed out, working out that, once again, Billy had fallen for the unattainable older woman.

Well, at least it was better than his last major crush, which was on his eighteen-year-old neighbour, who was blissfully unaware of his existence.

"I know, but I'm not going to let that put me off. I really want to get to know this girl," he sighed wistfully.

"What – and use up all your allowance buying sports socks?" I teased him.

"No. Well, not necessarily," he waffled, wriggling about on the seat. Last time I saw anyone do that, it was Rolf, when he had worms.

"So, what are you going to do?" I asked. "Stand outside the shop window, steaming up the glass as you stare in at her?"

"Aww, don't give me a hard time about it, Ally!" he whimpered.

I squirmed a bit myself on the bench. I didn't think I'd given him a hard time, and I hadn't meant to be mean, but *I* always tease him and *he* always teases me. That's what we do. That's the way it's always been since we were in nursery together.

"What's wrong with you?" I mumbled, feeling kind of hurt.

"Well, I – I never get it together with girls, do I?" Billy sighed.

I wasn't going to argue with that. Sweet as Billy was, he was still a snog-free zone. Not that I'm any big expert on that myself – not like Kyra – but at least my few rotten dates with Keith Brownlow once upon a time resulted in a couple of (not-so-hot) snogs.

"And I'm fed up of bottling it when it comes to chatting girls up."

Wow – he really did sound down about it.

"But I just feel like maybe this time, I can do it. If *you* help…"

I was feeling so sorry for my sad-boy buddy that I nearly missed that last bit.

"Help?" I squeaked, making the dogs stop their game of Lick-Chase for a second to stare at me. "What do you mean?"

"Aww, please, Ally!" he turned and looked at me beseechingly.

Now there were four sets of hound-dog eyes fixed on me.

"What can *I* do?" I asked him

Whoo, what a *strange* idea – helping Billy snag himself a date. But what was the difference between me helping him out, or Sandie, or Chloe, or one of my other friends if they fancied someone?

"Come with me to the sports shop after school on Thursday!" Billy explained, his words tumbling out fast. "I feel stupid going in there on my own again! And you're really smart! You'll be able to suss out loads of things about her that I'm too dorky to figure out! And then once I know more stuff about her, maybe I can come up with something to say to her, and then maybe I could ask her out! I mean, *some*time, not straight away! But I could end up with a girlfriend and it would be all down to you because you're my best friend and you did me this brilliant favour!"

He was rushing ahead of himself, old Billy-o. It's a wonder he hadn't added that I could be a bridesmaid at their wedding and that he'd name their first *kid* after me, whether it was a boy *or* a girl. But it was a pretty nice compliment, him thinking I could help somehow. And it was quite good fun hearing him call himself a dork – it saved me doing it. Even if the whole idea of setting my Billy up with another girl was triple-strength weird...

"OK," I heard myself saying. "I'll come along with you on Thursday. But I'm not promising anything. I'm not the fairy godmother of hot dates, y'know."

"Course! I mean, brilliant!" Billy grinned, so wide his smile reached his ears.

"You've got to promise me one thing, though," I said, fixing him with a serious stare.

"What?" he asked, his smile nervously slipping.

"When we walk in that shop, you'd better not be wearing a bra on your head. The girls just don't go for it – *warrrggghh!*"

Never tease a boy in love if you don't want to get a Chinese burn.

Chapter 2

AND ONE, AND TWO, AND THREE...

"*Unnnnggggg-fffff...*"

I wished I wasn't making that noise. It was really stupid.

"*Unnnnnggg-fffffff...*"

Look – there it was again, and I'd been trying extra hard not to do it.

"*Unnnnnggggg-ffff...*"

OK – that was it. Enough with the stupid noises and the exercise for one day.

"Toast?" said Dad, tantalizingly holding out a plate to me as, exhausted, I flopped down on the sofa in front of the Sunday omnibus of *EastEnders*.

"No thanks," I wheezed, trying to stick to my resolution of cutting out snack attacks and starting to exercise more.

(I was secretly hoping that a couple of days of sit-ups and nothing in-between meals would instantly give me a supermodel-flat stomach, so I could bottle out of Rowan's weirdo belly-dancing class on Tuesday night with a clear conscience.)

"Sure?" Dad asked again, wafting a plateful of great smells under my nose. "Me and Tor got the munchies, and I've made far too much for just the two of us."

I stared at the hot buttery hunks of toast and felt my resolve wobble as much as my squashy tum.

"That half is honey on toast," Dad pointed out, "and that half's your favourite – peanut butter on toast..."

Without my brain even agreeing to it, my hand shot out and grabbed a great big slice.

"Thanks, Dad," I mumbled through a full mouth.

"Anyway, Ally Pally – I don't want you getting all funny about food, just 'cause you want to get fitter," Dad tried to say casually, so he didn't sound like he was about to give a lecture.

(When I'd come back from the park and promising Billy big favours, I'd found out that Rowan had told Dad all about my tummy traumas and our little outing to the dance class. I only hoped she could keep her trap shut and resist telling Linn. I couldn't *stand* the shame of Linn sniggering over it with The Lord of Loveliness himself, Alfie... Oh, yes, in case you were wondering – I'd given up on giving up fancying boys. Well, how could I desert Alfie after all this time?)

"I won't," I assured Dad as I chomped.

"And you *have* done a lot of exercise today, after all," he continued. "I mean, you walked the dogs up at Ally Pally, and you've just been doing sit-ups, so you *are* allowed to eat to make up for all the calories you've burned off!"

I nodded, since I was in the middle of a swallow.

"So how many sit-ups did you do just now?" he asked, all interested.

I looked at his kind, trusting face.

"Ten," I blurted out.

"Um, ten … well, that's a start!" he tried to say encouragingly, even though I could tell that he thought it was a bit feeble.

Just as well I didn't say it was really only *three*.

"So where *is* the boy with the munchies?" I asked, in an equally feeble attempt to change the subject.

"Uh … I don't know," Dad replied, furrowing his dark brows together, so one hairy eyebrow nearly bashed into the other. *"Toooorrrr!* Toast's readddddyyyyy!"*

Both of us expected a thundering of small boy trainers, but the only pattering of tiny feet came in the form of a very excited Rolf and Winslet, who magically understand Human-Speak when any food words are involved.

"Hold on – he's probably out in the garden. I'll go and get him," I said, pushing myself up off our marshmallow of a sofa. "Where's Tor, Rolfy? You going to show me where Tor is? Fetch! *Fetch!*"

Rolf happily padded alongside me, as I made my way through to the kitchen and out of the open back door. But to be honest, I think he was less concerned with being a search-and-rescue dog and more interested in the idea that he might somehow wangle a chunk of the toast in my hand.

"Tor?" I called out, even though I could see straight away that my brother wasn't out in our big, green, gently overgrown garden.

In fact, the only sign of life was a grumpy cat that wasn't Colin sitting hunched up on the wall.

"Seen Tor?" I asked Fluffy, who just gave me a typically huffy Fluffy stare. (Whoever named that cat originally got it *so* wrong, I'm telling you. Her personality is about as fluffy as *concrete*.)

Kicking a half-inflated football off the path (which Rolf immediately started chewing, since nothing else edible seemed to be coming his way), I walked up to the shed at the back of the garden – otherwise known as the Animal Hospital (sickly residents at present: none). But before I reached it, I heard a familiar voice coming from … somewhere or other.

"Tor...?" I muttered, standing tippy-toes on a wobbly pile of old bricks in the flower (and weed) bed.

Watched by a mildly curious Fluffy, I leaned on the top of the garden wall with my elbow and peeked into the neighbouring garden (a neater version of ours, without the rusty swing, the never-empty clothes line and the sneaky weeds pretending to be flowers). And though I couldn't see anyone through the open patio doors, I was pretty sure that my not so long-lost little brother's voice had come drifting out from there.

Looked like I was about to introduce myself to our new neighbours, whether I wanted to or not.

And you know something? I really wanted to. Like I said, I'd given up on giving up on fancying boys. And that didn't just mean Alfie ... maybe the new neighbours *did* happen to have a gorgeous teenage son tucked away in there – and going in search of Tor was my perfect excuse...

Chapter 9

PET-BOY TO THE RESCUE!

A gorgeous teenage boy moving in next door? I should be so lucky.

As I soon discovered, the big house next door was home to Michael, Harry and Tabitha – as well as a tankful of tropical fish – and not one of them was gorgeous, teenage, or, indeed, a boy.

Pah.

The house itself felt back to front – where our kitchen was, next-door had a big, sunny living room. The furniture was about a million miles away from what we had, too – instead of quirky (i.e. rickety) antiques (i.e. second-hand stuff), it was all low, black leathery, super-classy stuff that must have cost an arm and three legs. Instead of all our nice, junky arty, crafty ornaments etc. (we could set up shop with the amount of candlesticks, Indian cushions, paintings and pottery bits we have littering every spare surface), here, it was all ... empty. Or "minimalist", as Linn would have described it.

She'd love this place! I thought, as I gazed round the clutter-free room.

Of course, the one thing that *was* truly naff was the hideous flowery blue wallpaper – a little reminder of the frosty-faced Fitzpatricks.

"It's very nice!" I said, trying not to move about and make farty, squelchy noises on the leather sofa.

"Thank you! We'll have to get round to changing this *awful* decor, of course," smiled the friendly-looking, middle-aged bloke coming out of the kitchen with a glass of something fizzy for Tor. "Sure you don't want a juice or something, Ally?"

"No, I'm fine, Mr ... um..."

"Michael. Just call me Michael," he said reassuringly, as he settled himself on the arm of a big leather chair.

The big leather chair where my little brother was sitting, with a huge grin on his face and most of his legs obscured by a very large, very hairy, white Persian cat.

Here's the deal: Tor is pootling about in the back garden with the dogs, till Dad gets the munchies together. But Pet-Boy's ears prick up when he hears some cat-yodelling – a sure sign that a kitty fight is imminent. He scrambles up the garden wall, and spots our very own Fluffy in the neighbours' garden, all puffed up like a furry black and white balloon with claws, and intimidating some nervous-looking new cat on the block (the white purry cushion he's now got on his lap). So Pet-Boy rushes to the rescue, chucking himself over the wall, and shooing Fluffy back to her own territory. Just as he's giving the ancient, dribbly old Persian a bit of an it'll-be-OK cuddle, out comes "Michael" who's seen the whole drama and wants to thank his new neighbour for helping Tabitha (the old lady cat).

And in the ten minutes since he performed his heroic feat, Tor – according to "Michael" – has never shut up. Which for Tor is seriously weird.

"So you're the youngest of Tor's sisters?" Michael flummoxed me by asking.

"Um, yes..." I nodded, shooting a look at Tor. Who just sat beaming happily.

"Tor's been telling me that all the animals like your attic bedroom, Ally. He says there's always a few of them sleeping in corners. Except for maybe the fish and the stick insects, eh, Tor?"

Tor burst into over-enthusiastic giggles, as if that was the funniest thing he'd ever heard in his seven-year-old life. He was gazing up at this bloke Michael as if he was Santa Claus or something.

What *was* with all this? Why did Tor look so ... besotted?

I soon found out.

"Ally – Michael is…" Tor suddenly began, gulping mid-sentence in his excitement, "…a vet!"

Well, that made a lot of things instantly clear. The biggest deal for most kids would be getting taken to DisneyWorld, or being given a fancy new computer with a stash of games or something, but for Tor, having a vet move in next door was like having all his birthdays rolled into one.

"So, Tor was telling me that your father has a bike-repair shop around the corner?"

What was Tor like? How had he managed to give Michael our entire family history in the space of ten minutes when his teacher at school said he can sometimes go for ten days without talking?

"Yes, it's just a couple of streets away," I nodded on auto-pilot.

"Well, that's good to know!" said Michael brightly. "Harry's got a mountain bike which needs the gears fixed – I'll tell him where he can take it!"

Hmm. This was all very polite, but I knew I should be getting back home; all Dad had seen of me was a blur running through the hall towards the front door, yelling, "I know where Tor is! Back in two seconds!"

"Tor, we should get going," I pointed out, pushing myself off the squelchy sofa.

"Of course!" said Michael, getting to his feet. "Your mum might be wondering where you are, Tor!"

For a second there, Tor looked kind of odd. I guess he was waiting for me to do the explaining. But, wow – at last, there seemed to be at least one thing in our lives that Tor *hadn't* managed to blurt out.

"Our mum's abroad," I said hurriedly, holding out my hand for Tor. "She's doing charity work."

I wanted to get out of there fast – Michael seemed smart and might ask questions I couldn't answer, like where she was exactly and what charity she was supposed to be working for. I didn't ever get asked those questions by anyone at school – so many people had parents who'd split up that it wasn't unusual, and anyway, the etiquette at school was always that no one nosied into anyone else's situation, in case it got them upset.

"OK, say bye to Tabitha and … Michael," I told Tor, stumbling over using this grown-up guy's first name.

It felt as bizarre as the idea of calling Billy's mum Sharon to her face, or calling my teachers anything but Mr and Mrs Whatever.

"Bye, Michael! Bye, Tabitha! Bye, fish!" Tor sing-songed.

"Thanks again for rescuing Tabitha, Tor!" said Michael, showing us to the front door and giving my brother a big thumbs-up. "Bye! And bye to you, Ally! Or do you prefer Alexandra?"

"Ally is fine," I replied, giving my blabbermouth brother's hand a knuckle-crunching squeeze.

"I'm glad Michael is so nice—"

"*And* a vet," Tor interrupted Dad.

"Yes…" Dad agreed, tightening his jaw a little. "I'm glad Michael is such a nice man *and* a vet, but you really shouldn't have gone into his house like that, Tor. Not till we all get to know him better."

"But he has a cute cat!" Tor protested, looking stunned at Dad's reaction, now that I'd dragged him back through from next door and sat him down on the sofa, in front of the stone-cold toast.

"Yes, I *know* he has a cute cat…"

Dad's voice had an edge to it, as if he was half-aggravated and half-trying not to laugh while he gave Tor this mini-lecture.

"Can I go now?" Tor asked, scuffing his feet on the living-room carpet. "I've got to do a poem."

"Tor, what we're talking about is kind of important," Dad stressed. "More important than a poem right now…"

"Hi! It's me!" we all heard Linn call out as the door slammed closed.

It was the perfect distraction for Tor – he bounced off the sofa and out of the room in quadruple-fast time.

"Tor!" Dad called out, as we heard him thumping his way up the stairs.

"It's homework!" we heard him call down, justifying his sudden poetic urge.

"That went well!" I grinned cheekily at Dad. "Were you any better at the sex-education talk this morning?"

"Probably not," Dad grinned ruefully back.

"What's going on?" asked Linn, dumping a bag on the floor and flopping on to the sofa. She'd been to a party the night before and stayed over at her friend Nadia's, missing out on the excitement so far today.

"Ally'll fill you in," said Dad, getting to his feet. "I'd better go and check that Tor got the Stranger Danger message…"

"So?" Linn yawned at me, once Dad had started thundering his way upstairs.

It had obviously been a good party. Unlike Billy's.

"Uh, let me see…" I said, rubbing my chin thoughtfully. "One of Tor's mice had babies; Dad tried to explain *why* the mouse had babies; Tor wangled his way into the house next door; Dad's just been trying to explain *why* that was maybe not such a smart idea till we got to know the neighbours better, and … that's about it. Enough?"

"*More* than enough," Linn yawned again.

Wow – it definitely *must* have been a good party. Specially since Linn had been too tired to straitjacket her hair into its regulation tight, stubby ponytail today. In fact, her blondey-fair bob had almost started to go a bit curly, and Linn – the Queen of Blow-Drying – *never* allowed that to happen.

"Didn't you get your hands on a hairdryer this morning?" I asked, checking out the definite waviness going on around her face.

"No – Alfie couldn't find it."

My heart stopped; I swear it did.

And by the look on Linn's face, so did hers, as soon as she realized what she'd said.

"*Alfie?!*" I squeaked, feeling flushed at the very idea of standing near him, never mind staying *over* with him. "What happened to Nadia?! You were meant to be staying the night at Nadia's!"

"She was there too!" Linn blurted out sheepishly. "It's just that we stayed the night at Alfie's, not Nadia's, 'cause Alfie's parents are away on holiday, and we didn't have to worry about how late we came in. Oh, Ally, please don't tell Dad! I know he's cool and everything, but it might freak him out too much, me staying over at Alfie's!"

"No – no, of course," I stuttered, still in shock at the idea of seeing Alfie all sleepy from his bed … his fair hair all tousled … and maybe only wearing a T-shirt and boxer shorts…

"You know how it is," Linn kept chattering at hyper-speed. "It's sometimes hard for people to get their heads round the fact that a boy and girl can just be friends. Even Dad… I mean, I know he likes Alfie, but he might not be too crazy at the idea of me staying the night at his."

Hey, I understood what she was talking about. It was the whole "Can Boys and Girls Really Be Just Friends?" debate all over again, and Linn was right there on my side. It wasn't often the two of us had stuff in common (just about as often as you see a dodo flapping past the window), but this was definitely one of those moments.

"Course I understand," I told her. "It's just like me and Billy. We're just friends, even if Kyra did go and say he fancied me. And anyway, that's not true, 'cause he's in love with this other girl, and he wants me to help him find out more about her, and I'm going to help him, even though it's a bit weird. Uh, not that I'm jealous – it's just weird.

Though it shouldn't be – 'cause it wouldn't be weird if it was Kellie or Salma asking me. It's just because it's Billy, and it's this really pretty girl. Well, he *says* she's really pretty, but I don't know if she is. Not that I *care* if she is..."

I fizzled out at that point, knowing that I'd sounded like a jibbering idiot somehow, when all I'd wanted to do was have a one-to-one, we've-got-something-in-common conversation with my big sis.

Only something told me – maybe the way she was staring at me like I was a fruitbat – that it hadn't quite worked.

"What's up with you, Ally?" she frowned. "Have you got a crush on Billy or something?"

Aaarrrggghhhh!

Why did I ever think I could talk emotionally on the same wavelength as Linn? I take back what I said earlier – me and her? Us having something in common was a *lot* more rare than a sighting of a dodo flapping past the window, a *lot* more rare. Maybe as rare as *two* dodos flapping past the window...

Chapter 10

THE GRACEFUL ART OF WIBBLE-WOBBLING

Talk about bad timing.

Grandma had just made an amazing pasta and cheese thing ("Ricotta tortelloni – I saw that lovely Jamie Oliver make it on some TV programme," she explained, dolloping the great-tasting splodge out on to our mismatched plates). Trouble was, I couldn't face eating it – all because nerves and lack of time were getting in the way. It was Tuesday night, and in less than twenty minutes' time, some teacher in some draughty church hall was seriously expecting me to wiggle my bits for the world to see. Or at least for everyone else in the class to see, and that was scary enough.

And there was another reason I wish I could have eaten the cheesy pasta stuff – it was the last Grandma-made meal we'd be getting for a while. She was taking off to Cornwall the next day to visit some old buddy of hers for a week or so.

The way I saw it, it really wasn't fair of Grandma to go. It wasn't that I didn't want her to have a good time, and it wasn't that I minded taking over more chores during the week, like hoovering or doing the laundry or helping Tor with his homework. It was just the fact that Grandma being away meant we'd all have to suffer from an extra helping of Rowan's terrible cooking. But there was nothing I could do about that – not even offer to take Ro's turn for her. We were a fair family, as Dad liked to put it, so it was only "fair" that Rowan got a chance to give us all food poisoning that bit more often.

"Ally, dear – please try and eat *something*," Grandma advised me, looking at me through her gold-rimmed glasses. "I don't want you falling over during this ... *class* of yours."

Oh dear – from the way she said "class" you could tell she was slightly disapproving of what Rowan and I were up to, and I knew it was because she had this idea that was somehow all too *rude*.

"By the way, what exactly will you be wearing at this *class*?" Grandma continued, making the word sound super-seedy.

"*I* know, *I* know!" Linn grinned, sticking her hand – and fork – up in the air.

(You guessed it – Rowan hadn't been able to stop herself blabbing to Linn about the belly-dance doodah. Thank you, Rowan. *Very* much.)

"It's all spangly jewelled bras and rubies in your belly buttons, isn't it?" Linn sniggered at her own non-funniness.

"No!" I squeaked in horror, then shot her a look that said, "I know your little secret about Saturday night – so quit teasing or I'll tell!"

Not that I would have, since I'm not a blabbermouth and since I knew she hadn't done anything really wrong. But it was handy to know that Linnhe Love – Miss Perfect – wasn't quite so perfect after all, and that she *knew* I knew.

Anyway, so much for spangly bras and jewelled bits – I was already wearing what I'd be dancing in: a pair of running trousers and a vest top. With not a spangle in sight. And no one was going to get the chance to glimpse my flubbery tummy, let alone stick anything in my belly button.

"Well, we won't be getting dressed up in anything spangly *yet*," Rowan shocked me by answering. "When Von spoke to the teacher on the phone, she just said to wear something casual first time. If we like it and want to come back, *then* we can start dressing up more..."

Uh, excuse me? It seemed like my middle sister had given me the edited highlights when it came to our exercise outfits. When we'd talked about it yesterday, she hadn't said anything about dressing up more, later on. (Probably, I realized, as I watched her shoot me a guilty sideways glance across the table, because she didn't want to scare me off. And she'd have been right.)

But there was no *way* I'd ever turn up to a class all fancy-pantsed up and standing out like a spangly sore thumb. No *way*.

Twenty minutes later, I was standing out like a very *underdressed* sore thumb, looking washed-out and feeling flat in my grey top and trousers in amongst a tropical garden's worth of colours. And that's not to mention the glittery bits that seemed to glint from everyone's hips and wrists.

Standing in that church hall was a bit like being in Rowan's room, minus the fairy lights.

OK, so there were no spangly jewelled bras (just a lot of cropped tops) and no rhinestones in anyone's belly buttons that I could see (although there were a couple of people wearing belly chains – including my sister). What there was was lots of long flowy skirts in Indian silks and chiffons, lots of bangles and beads, and most interestingly, these weird fabric belts with rows and rows of coin-things sewn on that tied around the hips and covered everyone's bums. They made a lot of noise, ker-tinkling away as everyone bumbled about and chatted. God knows how loud they'd be when everyone started actually *dancing*.

And what a total racket they must make when you're trying to go to the loo…

As my panicking mind began wandering off into its own dopey universe, Rowan pulled me back to reality. The reality that I was very probably about to make a fool of myself any minute now.

"It's exciting, isn't it?" Rowan whispered, all goggle-eyed.

Exciting? It was so exciting that I felt like I was going to be *sick*.

It was all right for Rowan and Von – they weren't the youngest person in the room, by about a million years. All the women there were … well, *women*. Even in their fancy-dress get-ups, they all looked like they were responsible adults with jobs and mortgages and kids (and grandkids in the case of a couple of them). Meanwhile, *I* sometimes still *shopped* in Gap Kids.

"Ladies!" said someone very elegant and glamorous, breaking away from a huddle of jingling women and heading in our direction. "Lovely to see new faces!"

I glanced behind us to see the "ladies", but there was nobody there – just the back wall of the room where we'd bagsied our places.

"My name's Gloria, and I take the class," Glittery Gloria smiled in turn at me, Rowan and Von, with her sheeny-shiny mulberry-stained lips.

She *had* to be the teacher – her shimmery gold skirt, waist-length black hair and kohl-rimmed eyes made her stand out as the most exotic person in the room.

"Now, have any of you done any belly dancing before? Any of you got any physical problems or injuries I need to know about?"

Rowan and Von managed to squeak out shy little "no"s. When *I* tried, no sound came out, so I just mouthed the word "no".

(Von – I was quite interested to see – was suddenly not quite her cool, aloof self, no matter how uninterested and casual she'd tried to come across when we'd met her outside, just a few minutes ago. Her own black-eye-linered eyes were wide and nervous-looking. Hurrah! She was human after all!)

"Well, don't worry," Gloria assured us, gold bracelets clinking at her wrists as she smoothed back her amazing hair. "We do a gentle warm-up first, then I'll get you started on some basic steps. After that, I'll move my other ladies on to a routine we're working on for a show we're performing soon—"

Eeek! A show! A performance! What had I started?

"—but of course, I won't be throwing you in at the deep end with that – I'll just come over and show you some more standard steps. OK?"

OK.

Heart rate slowing down.

Panic subsiding…

And so we were off, in a mind-jangling hour-long blur of shaking, wibbling and wobbling.

Those are not proper technical terms in belly dancing, just in case you were wondering. If you want me to get all technical on you, then here's a few tortures – sorry, *moves* – I managed to remember the names of:

First, there was the HIP DROP, where you stand with one foot flat and the other arched up on the toes, dropping one hip down sharply in time to the music. I thought I'd got the hang of it till Gloria came over and told me I was doing…

The HIP LIFT: where you stand the same way, but whip your hip upwards instead. (The minute we started that, my hip decided it preferred the hip *drop*.)

The HIP CIRCLE was OK, but I didn't feel too gorgeous, standing there sticking first my bum and then my jelly belly out into this big arc. But it was a lot better than the…

HIP THRUST, where you have to, er, thrust your hips forward. (Try doing *that* and not giggling. I think Grandma would have *fainted* if she saw us doing that one.)

By the time we'd got ourselves through that lot, I was beginning to wonder why it was called belly dancing and not *hip* dancing.

But we weren't finished, there – oh no. There was more, like:

The SHIMMY, where you have to do this shivery-shaky thing with your bum, like there's an earthquake happening down your trousers. But I was a tremor-free zone, and only managed to get a stitch.

Then there's the EGYPTIAN WALK, a walk where you shimmy a bit too. Yeah, *right*. I never knew Egyptians walked like shaky-bottomed ducks. Couldn't do it. Didn't know if I actually *wanted* to.

The last thing we learned – or didn't, in my case – was the CAMEL, a truly amazing whole body snaky thing (what it had to do with camels I couldn't figure out). Sadly, even without seeing myself, I could tell I was moving more like a wooden rocking horse than a sinewy snake.

But finally, *finally*, there came a move I could do. It was called … GOING HOME.

"Wasn't that amazing!" Von enthused, as

everyone clapped at the end of the class, for some unknown reason.

Von said that directly to Rowan, not to me, of course, but then I *am* mostly invisible to Von.

"Yeah! I can't wait till next week!" Rowan sighed blissfully. "I'm really going to get dressed up for that!"

While the two of them yakked away, I grouchily pulled on my trainers, saying nothing. I'd felt about as graceful as a pot-bellied pig in *clogs* all through that, and speaking of bellies, from where I was hunched down, my very own squishy stomach was still very much *there*. Grrr...

But you know what? Looking around at all the women in the class as they untied their glittery coin belts and got changed into their own boring everyday clothes (and trying not to look like some ogling weirdo while I did it), two things suddenly struck me. First, everything turned from dayglo to dull, as the spangles were swapped for T-shirts and jeans and stuff, and second, apart from Her Glitterness Gloria (and Von and my sister), there wasn't a textbook slim-line body in the room.

In fact, there were loads of different shapes, sizes and squashy bits in here – I hadn't noticed before, due to panic blindness and the dazzle of the fancy-dress outfits.

At the end of the lesson, when Gloria had said, "That's all for tonight, ladies, thank you!", I'd automatically thought, "Yes! I'm free! I never have to do this ever again!" But hey, maybe there *was* a point to coming back next week, after all. Next to some of the jelly bellies on show here, mine was a mere blip. A *junior* jelly belly.

"Do you fancy coming back to mine for a coffee?" I heard Von say.

You know something? For one, stupid second, I thought she might be including me in that invite. But one glance at her and I saw straight away that her eyes were fixed very firmly on Rowan.

"You don't mind, do you, Ally?" Rowan turned and smiled at me apologetically.

"Nope," I shrugged, trying to look casual, even if every muscle in my abdomen hated me for what I'd just put them through. "I'll be fine on my own."

Anyway, I wouldn't be on my own. Just down the road from the church there was a late-night grocer's, and I could hear a family-size bag of sour cream and chive kettle crisps calling my name from here...

Chapter 11

MICE AND MUDDLES

It was Wednesday, I'd finished school for the day, and I'd just turned down the chance of goofing along to Kentucky Fried Chicken with Salma and Jen and the others.

Normally, I hate to miss out on one of these girlie gatherings, but since Grandma had scooted off on her holidays, I had to act the responsible big sister and take my turn picking up Tor from school. Well, not exactly – the arrangement was that he'd hang out at his friend Freddie's house for the time in-between *his* school coming out and me finishing mine.

Anyway, I was pretty glad of the excuse. If my muscles hated me after belly dancing last night, they wanted to hang, draw and *quarter* me today. During class, my mates hadn't really noticed the fact that I was walking like a geriatric penguin, but I knew it was going to be hard to avoid their scrutiny if I winced every time I reached over for my Coke. And there was no way I was going to tell my friends *why* I was wincing. I just couldn't handle the stick I'd get. I mean, Chloe and everyone, they can tease you to death just for coming to school with a price sticker still on the sole of your shoe or having a squint hair-parting or something.

Sandie knew, of course. I'd told her on the way to school on Monday, and sworn her to secrecy. Not that I had to – she was always one hundred per cent reliable when it came to being loyal and trustworthy. It's just a pity she was *minus* one hundred per cent interested in coming along to belly dancing with me and trying it out.

"*Oooh, noooo!*" she'd squeaked, as if I'd suggested she ran naked down Crouch End Broadway singing Westlife songs at the top of her voice.

"Please! It could be fun!" I'd pleaded, trying to convince myself as well as her.

"*Oooh, noooooo!*" she'd giggled, hiding her face with her hands.

"There's not going to be any boys there, if that's what you're worried about! No one will see you!" I'd tried one last time.

"*Oooh, noooo!*"

That was a definite no, then.

I did think of bribing her, offering to pay for the two of us to see a movie of her choice (with hotdogs and popcorn thrown in, natch) *and* a long-term loan of my T-shirt with the star on it that she really likes, but I knew it was pointless. Sandie's shy, and like a lot of shy people she has this really stubborn streak. So once she'd said "*Oooh, noooo!*" a few times, it was obvious that I wasn't going to get her to budge.

One thing I hadn't decided yet was whether or not I'd go back next week. I mean, I did like the fact that I looked pretty slinky-malinky next to some of the stomachs on show in there, but it was just the thought of all those silly shimmies and camels ... not to mention the *supremo* silly hip thrust.

How did it go again? I mused to myself as I took the turning into the road that went past Tor's school. *Step and* thrust *that hip, step and* thrust *that hip, step and* thrust *that hip...*

It took me a couple of minutes to realize what I was doing – long enough for puzzled old ladies to peer through their net curtains at the freak on their street. Oh, *and* Freddie's mum.

I waved back at her and prayed she hadn't seen what I was doing, although I knew – as sure as snot is green – that she had.

"Hello, Ally! Come on in!" Mrs Jackson urged me at the door.

"No – it's OK – I'm in a bit of a rush," I lied. (A rush to get home and *shoot* myself.) "Is Tor ready?"

"Sure," Mrs Jackson smiled broadly at me. Oh, yes, she'd seen. "Tor! It's your sister! Want to get your stuff together?"

From inside came the squeal of Tor and Freddie mucking around.

"Has he been OK?" I tried to ask conversationally, hoping my face wasn't as bright pink as it felt.

"Oh, he's been fine," Mrs Jackson beamed at me. "Tor is a *lovely* boy. And he let me read the *sweetest* poem he wrote. Oh, but there was something I meant to tell you..."

All thoughts of poetry forgotten, Mrs Jackson leant forward, throwing a quick glance behind her, to check the coast was clear of small boys.

"Well, dear, Tor seems to be a bit ... *muddled,*" she whispered.

"Muddled?" I shrugged, having not one, single clue what she was on about.

"I heard him telling Freddie something..."

Mrs Jackson was biting her lip; I wasn't sure if she was embarrassed, or simply trying not to laugh.

"It's just that I overheard your brother telling my Freddie about his mouse having babies," she continued to explain. "And the trouble is ... Tor

93

seems to think *ladies* have mouse babies too, only they turn into children later on."

"Huh?" I frowned.

"He says your father told him that," she hissed, as thundering footsteps approached.

"Hi, Tor!" I smiled down at my brother.

"Bye, Tor!" Mrs Jackson hugged him. "See you tomorrow, honey!"

It made me feel all churny again, seeing Tor get that big, cosy, mumsy cuddle from Mrs Jackson. Of course, me and my sisters and Dad and Grandma all give Tor hugs – *gallons* of hugs – but there was something specially *cosy* about that mumsy hug. Maybe it was the happy, contented grin on Tor's face, peeking out over Mrs Jackson's robust arms, that made me think that way.

"C'mon, Tor," I smiled, holding out my hand to him.

"Bye!" Tor waved at Mrs Jackson, who in return gave me a quick wink as we hurried away.

For a while, me and Tor stomped along the pavement in companionable silence. Then I decided I'd get him talking, starting with the poem, since that had to be a safe bet – and then I'd work up to the confusion about the lady-mouse-babies thing. Well, that was my plan, only I didn't get too far.

"Freddie's mum said you wrote a nice poem,"

I began, squeezing his hand. "Was that the one you were talking about at the weekend? The one you had to do for homework?"

Tor nodded, but said nothing. Hey, that wasn't exactly unusual.

"Did you do that poem all on your own, then?" I asked, checking the top of his head for a reaction.

I spotted a nod.

"Can I read it?"

Uh-oh – a shake of the head.

"Why can't I read it? You let Freddie's mum read it!" I said, pretending to be hurt.

Tor said nothing, only kept his gaze to the ground.

"Is it something … secret?" I guessed.

Tor sort of shrugged.

"Well, if Freddie's mum could read it, why can't I? Is it something rude about *me*?!"

I only said it to get Tor laughing, but it didn't work – he just kept staring down at the paving stones we were pounding over.

This wasn't getting us very far. If he wouldn't tell me about the poem then I couldn't even begin to get started on the business of ladies and mice babies…

I had to do something that would get his attention and get him out of this odd little mood he was in.

"Hey, Tor!" I grinned, waggling the hand that I was holding and forcing him to look round at me. "Watch this! D'you think I'm a good dancer? Huh?"

I hip *thrust*, hip *thrust*, hip *thrust* my way along the pavement, refusing to stop till I saw the smile break on Tor's face, followed by a grin, and then a full-blown snigger.

Making a fool of myself to make Tor laugh was fine by me – even if the queue of people standing at the bus stop on the opposite side of the road thought I was an absolute *nutter*.

After publicly (and willingly) embarrassing myself with my hip thrusting, and getting Tor to giggle, I'd decided to leave well alone and give up on trying to get him talking about his poem (not that it seemed that important) and mice babies (thought I'd leave that one to Dad). Instead, we just goofed around some more.

Me and Tor were in mid-Tigger song when we bumbled back to the house – after spending an hour at the playground in Priory Park – and found Dad home from work (no surprise), my sisters home from school (ditto) and Billy too (slightly surprising, since I hadn't been expecting him).

Billy and Dad were watching an animal

documentary in the living room, while Rowan clattered about in the kitchen, warbling along – out of tune – to the radio. There was no sign of Linn, apart from her bag and jacket in the hall, so I presumed she was up in her room at the top of the house.

"Hi, Tor! I'm taping this programme for you, so don't panic!" Dad smiled, pointing at the telly and Tor's *numero uno* favourite programme.

"What are you doing here?" I frowned down at Billy sitting on the sofa, even though I was pleased enough to see him.

"Just thought I'd come round and check that you were still OK for tomorrow," he said casually, while lifting his eyebrows up and down at me in some kind of hairy-eyebrowed morse code.

Wow, he was *definitely* keen on this girl in the sports shop if he'd trundled all the way over to mine just to make sure I hadn't forgotten about helping him spy on her.

"Uh-huh," I mumbled at him dubiously.

"Oh, Tor – you just missed Michael; he left this for you," said Dad, handing my brother a small booklet called *Caring for Mice*. "He says it's a thank you for rescuing Tabitha."

"Who's Michael? And who's Tabitha?" Billy asked me, as Tor roared and grabbed his present.

"Tabitha's a *cat*," I explained, before Billy got too excited and imagined Tabitha as some foxy, teenage girlie. Not that he'd be too interested; not now he was fixated on the Sports Shop Girl. "And Michael's the vet who's moved in next door. There's another guy living there too – Harry – but we haven't met him yet."

"Oh," mumbled Billy, probably losing interest fast in what I was saying. Vets and cats didn't really rate highly on his list of fascinations.

"By the way, you're staying for tea, aren't you, Billy?" asked Dad.

"Sorry, can't," Billy shook his head. "Just stopped over for a minute, just to remind Ally about ... this *thing*."

It wasn't like Billy to refuse food. I suspected that he probably *had* planned on hanging around and eating with us (like he regularly did), until he walked in and remembered Grandma wasn't on cooking duties this week. And the thing that probably reminded him of that was the smell of cabbage and burnt fish wafting from the direction of the kitchen, where Rowan was rustling us up tonight's gloop. Sorry, tea.

Then he jumped, suddenly aware that Tor was staring intently at him over the back of the sofa.

"Billy," said Tor.

"Yeah, what?" replied Billy, trying not to look unnerved by my little brother (except he always is).

"Do you want to come and see my baby mice?"

"Uh, no, it's all right," Billy shook his head. "I've got to go in a second. Really."

Tor shrugged, looking a bit stunned that anyone could refuse such a fantastic offer, and disappeared out of the living room, with his mouse book clutched in his hand.

I should have waited a second before I said anything, just to make sure Tor was out of hearing range, but I didn't. The chance to tease Dad about his failure to explain where (human) babies come from was just too funny.

"Dad! Did you fail biology at school or something?" I grinned, sitting myself down next to Billy on the sofa.

"Huh? No – why?" said Dad, bewildered.

"'Cause you've managed to *totally* confuse Tor!" I explained. "He thinks mummies have some kind of little mice too, only they turn into proper kids later!"

Billy snorted so loud I had to check he hadn't turned into a pig.

"Oh, *no*..." Dad groaned and laughed, putting his head into his hands. "God, your mother was always so much better at this stuff than me. Sometimes I just expect Tor to understand grown-up things, and I forget he's still just a little boy."

"I am *not* just a little boy!" said an indignant little boy in the doorway.

"Oh, Tor," said Dad, a little flummoxed at being caught out. "We only meant—"

"You shouldn't be such big ... fat ... know-alls!" Tor stumbled on, trying to find the right words to rage with.

No wonder he couldn't find them – Tor wasn't the kind of kid who ever lost his rag.

"And I *do* know the difference between mice babies and people babies!" he announced. "People babies ... don't have tails!"

"...or *fur*, or *whiskers*," Billy snickered.

I whipped Billy's baseball cap off his head and hit him with it. Even though I was on the verge of giggling myself, I didn't want Tor to think any of us were laughing at him.

Oops. Too late.

"Don't laugh!" he blinked furiously at the three of us, going pink around the edges with pure frustration.

"We're not laughing," Dad assured him, pulling a mighty serious face.

"You were! And you shouldn't laugh at me –

I'm not a baby!" he ranted, his lower lip wobbling treacherously. "You think you're big and clever and that you know stuff, but you don't know everything! You don't know stuff about *me*!"

"Like what?" I quizzed him, feeling like a real ratbag for getting him so worked up.

"Like *secrets*!" Tor yelped, then stomped off out of the room in his first recorded strop in living memory.

"Ooh!" Dad whispered, widening his eyes at me and Billy. "I thought it was only two year olds and teenagers that had tantrums!"

"What do you think he meant, though?" I wondered out loud, hearing Tor's bedroom door slam shut. "What secrets?"

"Maybe he's been letting the boy and girl hamsters play together too, and he doesn't dare tell me..." Dad suggested.

I looked at Dad's face to see whether he was joking or not, and couldn't tell – his mouth might have been smiling but his eyebrows were frowning together like two hairy caterpillars squaring up for a fight. Seemed like he was just as puzzled as I was over Tor's strange little outburst.

All I could think of when it came to secrets was Tor going all coy on me about the poem he'd written; that and the fact that he'd sneaked that photo of Mum off the noticeboard and started carrying it around with him.

But that couldn't have anything to do with anything, could it?

"Tea's ready!" Rowan called through from the kitchen, above the blare of the radio.

"Got to go," said Billy hurriedly, before my dad press-ganged him into sharing our food.

And pulling his cap on, Billy shot off, leaving us to the mystery of Tor's strange secrets and what exactly Rowan's meal was supposed to be...

Chapter 12

THE BIG FAVOUR GETS BIGGER...

"You didn't tell me you were bringing Spook-kid!" mumbled Billy, giving Tor a wary sideways glance.

It was Thursday – Billy's Big Favour Day. I'd just picked Tor up from Freddie's, and we'd legged it up to Muswell Hill Broadway to meet up with lover-boy and help him with his quest for a hot date.

But typically, after a speedy uphill hike through Ally Pally park to get here, me and Tor had been left standing outside M&S – my designated meeting place with Billy – for what felt like *weeks*. Tor kept getting bored and scooting along the Broadway as far as the nearest side street that slipped steeply southward, just so he could stare at the awesome views right over London from there.

And that's what he was doing when Billy finally came mooching along the road, ambling like a cross between a homeboy and a *cowboy*, for goodness' sake.

"I *had* to bring Tor – it's my job to look after

him while Grandma's away, remember," I replied, giving Billy the once over and trying to figure out why – apart from the ridiculous walk he'd suddenly developed – he looked so weird. "And be extra nice to him – you saw how upset he was yesterday!"

Since his strop, Tor had gone into silent mode, as if he'd used up a week's worth of talking in that one little outburst. It didn't matter how much Dad, Linn, Rowan and I all tried to get round him during the evening, he wouldn't open up and tell us what was going on in his head, or what his "secrets" were. It had been the same today – he'd listen to me rabbiting on, but wouldn't say anything himself. I hadn't even been able to ask Mrs Jackson about the poem, 'cause he'd been standing there (silently), waiting for me when I went to pick him up.

"Hey!" I commented, suddenly figuring out why Billy was so late turning up. "You're not in your school uniform! You went home to change!"

The little poser! He'd wanted to get out of his boys'-school greys and into his trendiest clothes (in Billy's case, that means his baggiest beige skateboard cut-offs and a scuzzy, ancient Diesel T-shirt).

"Yeah, well—"

"Yeah, well, nothing!" I interrupted him. "And what's with your head?"

"What?" Billy blinked sheepishly, shrugging at me.

"Where's your baseball cap?"

"I don't wear baseball caps all the time, Ally!"

Liar. Unless he was in class (or busy wearing a bra bandanna – fnar!) he *always* had one of his *huuuge* collection of baseball caps stuck on his head.

"You do *so* wear baseball caps all the time!" I contradicted him. "Here, let's have a feel..."

Luckily, I was quicker than Billy was, and managed to swoop my fingers across the rigid mound of peaks his hair was moussed up into, just before he ducked out of reach.

"*Mousse!*" I giggled, pulling a face.

"*Wax,*" he mumbled, looking shifty around the edges.

"Are we going to see the girl Billy loves now?" asked Tor, suddenly appearing next to us.

Wow – it was great to hear his voice, to hear him speak a whole sentence.

"I don't *love* her!" Billy protested, going so pink his eyeballs practically flushed.

"Yes, Tor," I replied, ignoring Billy's cringing. "We *are* going to see the girl Billy loves. Isn't that nice?"

Billy was scowling at me so hard I knew he was regretting asking me for the Big Favour already...

* * *

"Um, excuse me, but are you Meera?" I asked, smiling shyly at the girl behind the counter.

Even if I did feel slightly shy, I was a million times more confident pulling this kind of stunt on Billy's behalf than doing anything like this for myself. You just need to look at the way I can't get past "Er … er … hi!" when I see Alfie to know that.

The girl – sorry, The Girl – narrowed her dark almond eyes at me.

"No, my name's Anita," she answered me, as she kept shooting her pricing gun at the pile of baseball caps on the counter in front of her.

Oh, how Billy (currently hiding in the swimwear section with Tor) would love to have her slide one of those on his head, I thought. If it would *fit*, of course, now that his hair had transformed into hedgehog-hard spikes.

"Oops! Sorry – you just looked like this new girl Meera that started in the year above me at school," I grinned apologetically at her. "At Palace Gates School."

Of course it was just a line. But it had got her to tell me her name. And more…

"I don't go to Palace Gates, I go to Fortismere," she answered me, blinking these massive Japanese-cartoon-style doe eyes at me.

Wow, no wonder Billy fell for her, hook, line

and sports sock. She was seriously pretty. And I felt seriously … almost … jealous there for a second. Not in a *fancying* kind of way, you have to understand. Just in a … well … I don't know. I couldn't figure it out.

"Ah, Fortismere," I muttered as casually as I could, pretending to check the price of some hideous yellow-lensed sunglasses beside the counter.

To be honest, I didn't know where to go from here. I'd found out her name, and what school she went to, and after that, my private-detective skills dwindled away. (Maybe because I was still trying to figure out what that weird jealousy pang was all about.) Which is where a much more skilled person in the field of detective work stepped in.

"Hello," said Tor, sidling up beside me, leaning his head on my arm appealingly and smiling up at Anita.

"Um, hello," Anita smiled back.

"Are you Prash's sister?" he asked her, giving her the full innocent, wide-eyed charm treatment. "Prash who lives in Redston Road?"

"No," she shook her head. "I don't have any brothers. Only big sisters. And I don't live down in Crouch End. I live up here in Muswell Hill. Beside the Golf Club."

"Oh..." murmured Tor. "That's right. You're too pretty to be my friend Prash's sister."

Where did Tor get this from? Not our sweet, ordinary goofy dad, that was for sure. Since when had my kid brother turned into a silver-tongued lady-killer?

Anita beamed first at Tor, and then grinned and raised her eyebrows at me. I didn't know what to say, apart from, "Sorry – my brother doesn't usually hit on girls older than six," when Tor was off again.

"Do you like mice?" he asked Anita out of the blue.

Anita looked flummoxed, half glancing over in the direction of her boss, who was busy putting a pair of Levi's on a dummy in the show window.

"Um ... I ... I suppose I quite like mice. Why?" she quizzed Tor.

"I have *lots* of baby white mice," he replied. "They're really cute. You could have one if you want..."

Before Anita got the chance to respond to Tor's totally resistible offer, a pair of white sports socks were flopped down on the counter.

"Can I pay for these, please?" asked Billy, blushing to the roots of his rigid hair.

It seemed that he'd got tired of hiding out in

the swimwear section while me and Tor hogged the attention of his dream girl.

"Sure," Anita nodded at Billy, turning her attention away from us and the pricing gun to Billy and the till.

"Bye!" I called out, grabbing my chance to yank Tor out of the shop before he helpfully offered the girl more of our pets.

"Bye!" she smiled, as she plopped the white sports socks into a small plastic bag.

As I walked out of the door, I was dying to look back at Billy, who I knew was probably dying to look back at me. But I managed to stop myself, and waited a few more minutes in the cool evening air outside to see how he'd reacted.

I didn't have to wait long.

"Ally! That was brilliant!" Billy crooned, as soon as he'd escaped the shop and hustled me a safe two doorways along the pavement. "Finding out her name and where she lives!"

"*I* did that bit!" Tor mumbled, loud enough for me to pick up, even if Billy didn't.

"Good!" I beamed at my friend. "Glad if I helped!"

"What did you think of her?" Billy asked, his eyes boring into mine as though it was the most important question in the cosmiverse.

"She's … nice!" I shrugged. "Seems really nice!"

Well, that much was obvious. Plenty of people would blank a seven-year-old kid, but Anita hadn't.

"And she nearly wanted a baby mouse!" Tor chipped in with his own character analysis.

"Er, OK," Billy frowned fleetingly at Tor. "So, Ally – could you … could you do one more thing?"

At the end of that sentence, he kind of crumpled in on himself, ending up looking like an apologetic hamster.

"Like what?" I frowned at him.

"Like … um … ask her if she wants to go out with me?" he blinked at me hopefully.

"No way! Absolutely no way!" I yelped, backing away from him.

Aargh! There was no way I could do someone else's asking for them! Eek! What a creepy idea!

Five minutes (and a lot of persuading later), I walked *out* of the sports shop and rejoined my brother. And Billy. Even if I didn't feel like acknowledging his existence after what he'd just got me to do.

My one way of getting back at Billy was to refuse to tell him what Anita had said until we'd got off the Broadway, through the twisty-turny covered alleyway and into the park.

"Oh, *YES!*" he'd called out, falling to his knees on the grass, once I finally spilled the beans.

Lucky him – a few centimetres over and he'd have landed in a pile of freshly deposited dog poo.

"Don't get *too* excited," I said in my flattest, most casual voice.

Casual? Who was I kidding? I wasn't feeling casual, I was stunned. Billy had struck lucky at last. I'd just asked some poor, unsuspecting girl if she could *possibly*, *maybe* not be *horrified* at the idea of going out with my friend, and she said … yes, OK, and scribbled her phone number on a piece of paper for me to give to him. Which I did now. Which made him roar even more, and fall flat on the grass with his arms outstretched.

"Why's Billy kissing the ground?" asked Tor, bemused.

"He's a big boy. Big boys are idiots. That what big boys do," I replied, folding my arms across my chest.

"Why?" frowned Tor, staring at Billy's prone figure, and watching him now kissing the piece of paper I'd just given him.

"I don't know," I shrugged. "Only promise me one thing, Tor. Promise me you'll go straight from being a cute kid to a nice grown-up like Dad. Don't do this dorky in-between bit, *please*."

But I didn't really mean it. Part of me thought it was really sweet the way Billy was acting. Please, *please* let some boy feel that excited about the idea of asking *me* out one day…

Then I spotted Tor's face and realized, for the second day running, that I'd said the wrong thing: this time, I'd called him a "kid", which wasn't a brilliant idea, considering that he was obviously really sensitive about that at the moment.

But luckily – and surprisingly – Billy got me out of that one fast.

"C'mon, Tor…" Billy suddenly roared, jumping to his feet. "Race you as far as the caff!"

And with that they were off, tearing over the grass with Tor yelping happily, while I carried on dawdling along the path, musing on the differences between boys and girls. I mean, if it was Salma or Kellie who'd just got a date with someone, their way of dealing with their excitement would be to talk over every, single, minute detail of it non-stop for *hours*. Whereas Billy had to burn off his excitement by bounding around the park like an over-enthusiastic labrador.

Not that I was complaining – it was great to see Billy mucking about with Tor. Normally he didn't have a clue how to act with him. And OK, so they might not be *communicating* exactly, but thundering around together like a pair of boisterous dogs was pretty good news.

For a few minutes, I lost sight of them both, as a bunch of trees got in the way. Then I turned a winding corner in the path and spotted Billy standing yakking to a couple of lads in the Muswell Hill School for Boys uniform, while Tor hung about, ignored now, by Billy's side.

Steven and Hassan – that's who the lads were.

"...yeah, and so Jez lent me it, but only if I give him a go of my new skateboard at the weekend," I heard Steven saying as I got closer.

The "it" had to be the PlayStation game he was clutching in his hands.

"So what've you been up to, Billy?" asked Hassan, giving me a quick nod hello – same as Steven – when I got up close.

(It was the first time I'd seen them since they were dressed in women's underwear and something told me that both boys were a teensy bit mortified...)

"Me?" said Billy, shrugging. "Not much."

"No?" chipped in Steven.

"Nah," Billy shook his head.

(Tor mooched off at that point to pat a nearby dog, and who could blame him, since the conversation was a lot less than thrilling.)

"Well..." Billy suddenly started up, "y'know, I've just been hanging out ... bought some stuff out of that sports shop on the Broadway ... got a date with this girl that works in there ... came down here to the park..."

I frowned at him. What was with the super-cool act? A minute ago, he was flat out on the grass, yelping with happiness. Fifteen minutes ago, and he was doing his crumpled hamster routine, *begging* me to ask Anita out for him. Now Billy was acting like the date with her was the most boring thing next to double maths.

"Whoa! Back up there!" gasped Hassan. "You've got a date ... with a girl?"

"Who is she?" asked Steven, positively gawping in wonderment.

"Nobody. Like I say, she's just this girl who works in the sports shop," Billy shrugged again. "I kind of fancied her, so I asked her out. That's all."

Would someone come and shove my bottom jaw up for me, please? I was gobsmacked! Why was Billy saying it like that? Why did he have to put a different spin on it when he was telling his buddies about what had just happened?

"Were you there, Ally?" Hassan asked me. "Did you see her?"

"Oh, yes," I nodded, firing a laser-eyed look at

Billy, who seemed to be deliberately avoiding my gaze.

"So, a date!" said Steven, shuffling uncomfortably.

"Yeah…" replied Billy nonchalantly, stuffing his hands in his pockets and nodding.

For a moment, all three boys sort of shuffled about, and said nothing.

See? This is what Rowan was going on about – boys not being able to show their emotions. All this stuff to do with Anita was zooming about in Billy's head, but he wouldn't *dream* of talking properly to his mates about it. *Oh*, no. *They* probably had a million questions running through their heads, but wouldn't dare ask them out loud. What were they like?

Speaking of emotions, I was almost tempted to give Billy a quick kick in the shins for being a liar-liar-pants-on-fire when it came to the small point of *who* exactly asked Anita out. Lucky for him that my parents brought me up to be a nice, non-kicking person.

Instead, I decided I'd be happier to go off and have an intelligent conversation with the most grown-up guy within shouting distance. Even if he was only seven years old and wasn't in the mood for talking.

"Bye – I've got to go," I waved at Hassan and Steven. "And I'll talk to *you* later, Billy!"

As I walked off to join Tor, Billy – who'd tried to act *so* tough in front of his mates – gave me the sheepiest of sheepish looks…

Chapter 13

SNEEZES AND SECRETS

God, don't you hate feeling like a fake?

I hadn't felt like a fake at eight o'clock that Friday morning, when I'd hazily made my way down to breakfast with a throat like I'd been gargling with broken glass or something and a nose that was dripping with snot.

"Anyone want a fried egg? This is hot enough to cook one on!" Dad had announced around the table, as he put his hand on my feverish forehead. "You and your germs aren't going anywhere today, Ally Pally!"

And so, while Linn, Rowan and Tor headed off to school and Dad went to the shop, I'd trotted back to bed with a hot-water bottle, a box of man-size tissues and a willing cat (Colin) to snuggle up to for comfort.

I slept and slept and slept till noon-ish, then woke up feeling ... fine.

Rowan came home at lunchtime and very sweetly offered to make me soup (from a tin, so

I was safe). I huddled up under a cosy blanket on the sofa when she brought my soup through to me on a tray, pretending to be more ill than I was, just because I felt so guilty at the idea of being such a skiver.

An hour later, once I had the house to myself again, I *really* started feeling like a big, fat fake. Apart from a slight dribble from my left nostril, all my yukky symptoms had vanished, and now I was seriously bored. *So* bored that I was in Dad's bedroom, entertaining myself (and a puzzled Rolf and Winslet) by trying out belly-dancing moves in front of the full-length wardrobe mirror, to the sounds of an old rock album of Mum's that was blasting out from the stereo in the living room downstairs.

(Not having any Arabic-y, Eastern-y belly-dancing music, I'd spent ages trawling through Mum and Dad's old records for something that might do. There was nothing in amongst Dad's crinkly old rock'n'roll stuff, so I'd picked a Led Zeppelin album from Mum's hippy rock-chick selection that had a track on it called "Kashmir", which sounded quite hopeful. It wasn't exactly the sort of thing that Glittery Gloria would have played in class – by about a million miles – but whatever, I could still do a hip thrust to it.)

But after twenty minutes of wiggling my way about the place, I was bored again, and the guilty feeling that I was skiving started seeping back. Then inspiration suddenly struck – thanks to Mum, kind of.

Sitting slouched and breathless of the edge of Dad's bed, I found myself staring up at her self-portrait, hanging right above the big, wooden headboard. Like all Mum's art, it's kind of hard to tell straight away what it is when you first look at it. I mean, this painting isn't as bad as the dolphin sculpture she did – the one that Kyra thought was a *slug* – you can definitely tell it's a woman, even if you don't recognize it as her. Apart from the eyes. Somehow her pale eyes are exactly the way they are in real life (or how I remember them). And right then, they seemed to be smiling down at me and telling me what I should do…

It felt strange, peeking into Tor's room when he wasn't there. The animals made me feel pretty guilty too – Buffy the rat, Stanley the goldfish, Mad Max and the other hamsters, Ronan the iguana, the (many) mice and gerbils (whose many names I couldn't remember), the tropical fish (ditto), the stick insects (ditto ditto) … all of them stopped snuffling or snoozling or wheel-surfing or whatever they were doing and stared out of their cages and tanks at me. I nearly jumped out of my skin when the pile of stuffed toys on the bed started moving – but it was only a cat that wasn't Colin, napping in disguise beside the soft-toy skunk.

"OK, Tor ... so where's this poem of yours?" I muttered, glancing round the cluttered room with its jungle green walls.

I looked on his desk, in amongst the school books, library books, colouring pencils and Beanie Babies, and didn't see any poems. On every surface, on every shelf, I found doodles and drawings, but no poems.

Course, it's probably in a schoolbook he's got with him now, I suddenly realized, sitting myself down on the edge of the bed and making Tor's mountain of soft toys – and the cat that wasn't Colin – jump.

Mum (weirdly enough) might have inspired me to come and search Tor's room for clues as to what was up with him, but it was a four-pawed family member that gave me my next bit of inspiration.

After pitter-pattering up the stairs, Winslet came padding into Tor's room, and then stopped dead when she saw me. Guilt was written across her fuzzy face – mainly because she had a Special Stolen Something in her mouth. I peered at it and saw it was a grey sock (Dad-sized rather than Tor-sized), and from the floppiness factor, it was definitely dirty rather than clean, so I didn't *desperately* feel like rescuing it. Sensing that I wasn't about to fight her for possession of the sock, Winslet padded on – watching me suspiciously with her dark beady eyes – and slunk under Tor's bed, after brushing past my pyjama'd legs and floppy dressing gown.

"So, Winnie – is this your latest hiding place?" I asked her, bending over and peering through my legs at the dark, fluff-hoarding underside of the bed.

Straight in front of me was Winslet, snuffling grumpily now that she realized her stash of stolen socks, feathers, old toilet rolls and assorted unidentifiable things had been sussed. But it wasn't just Winslet that stored stuff away from prying eyes. There, to my right, was an old margarine tub, still with its picture of a bright, happy sunflower on it. Normally – cross-my-heart-and-hope-to-die – I wouldn't have dreamt of noseying inside it, but right now I had a really strong feeling that it might help me find out if there really was anything wrong with Tor.

Tentatively, I scooped the plastic tub from under the bed, straightened up, and peeled the lid open. And inside was ... the picture of Mum in Canada (she looked tanned and happy, waving at us from inside a busy café that could have been anywhere, except for the *Here's me! All the way out in Toronto!* she'd scribbled on the back). Underneath the photo was a white piece of paper – one side ragged from where it had been ripped out of a jotter – folded over and over into a small, tight square. Bit-by-bit, trying to ignore the sense that I was snooping, I unravelled the sheet of paper and finally smoothed the whole thing out on my lap.

"The Mouse Mum" by Tor Love it said at the top of the page.

It was his poem. His secret showing-Mrs-Jackson-but-not-any-of-us poem. And this is what it said...

My favourite mouse had babies,
Not one, not three, but six.
When they go "squeak!" she feeds them,
And gives them cuddles, hugs and licks.

My mummy never licked me
And I don't think I ever went squeak!
But I wish that she could hug me,
Right now, right here, this week.

I can't tell my mum that I miss her
'Cause she lives far away
So instead I whisper to the mouse mum
That I miss my own mum every day.

Underneath, in red pen, his teacher had done a smiley face, and written "Very good!" beside it.

Very sad, more like.

Suddenly I started to feel shaky again, as it dawned on me that maybe Tor missed our mum more than any of us realized, and that this was his not-so-little secret...

I didn't wait till Dad got home to tell him what I'd found out.

Snotty-or-not, I just threw on some clothes and went rushing round to the bike shop.

"Hey, Ally Pally!" he called out, as I bolted through the shop door, sending the bell ding-a-ling-a-linging. "What's up?"

Luckily there were no customers – but even if there had been I would have probably just blabbered it all out in front of them anyway.

As I talked, Dad lay his tools down, perched his bum on saddle of the nearest bike, and ran his hands through his short, dark hair until it stuck up in spikes. By the time I'd finished, he looked like a perplexed punk with a mini-mohican.

"I'll talk to Tor tonight, at bedtime," said Dad, after frowning a lot and biting his lip. "I'll tell him we've read the poem..."

And that's when I realized I'd landed myself in it – Tor would *know* I'd been snooping in his room, and the last thing I wanted was to be his least favourite, most nosey sister.

After a few seconds of whirring panic in my head, I suddenly came up with a plan – OK, a *lie*.

"Dad, could you do me a favour?" I said to him.

"Sure," he shrugged. "What is it?"

"Can you tell him Winslet found the poem?" I suggested hopefully

"What – that Winslet prised open the lid, read the poem and came round here and *woofed* it at me?" Dad grinned.

"You *know* what I mean," I grinned back. "You could say Winslet must have dragged the tub out of his room—"

"—and I'd found it and wondered what it was and opened it. Yes, don't worry – one little white lie won't hurt."

The smile I gave him was a bit on the wobbly side; my cheek had developed a twitch – the twitch I always end up with when I get anywhere near a lie. Yep, other people get allergies to dairy products or peanuts or whatever – I'm allergic to lies.

Still, if it meant my little brother would still think I was a nice sister, it was worth all the twitching in the world.

Chapter 14

BURGERS AND BANGLES

My one-day bug had more or less vanished – the only sign left of it on Saturday was the few damp, snotty hankies crushed up in the pocket of my combats.

Weird though it was, I was pretty glad I'd had that bug. If I hadn't skipped a day at school, I wouldn't have gone rummaging in Tor's room and found the poem. And if I hadn't found the poem, I wouldn't have found out that Tor missed Mum as much as he did. Poor little sausage.

Once Dad had got Tor off to sleep the night before, he'd come downstairs and told us that he'd had a good (if one-sided) chat with Tor about Mum, telling him it was OK to feel sad that she wasn't around, and that he didn't have to hide it from all of us, 'cause we'd understand. Tor hadn't said much – just nodded and hugged Dad and an armful of soft toys while Dad tried to assure him that Mum would be home as soon as she could finish all her charity work, and that she loved him very much.

Me, Linn and Rowan felt pretty quiet ourselves after Dad said all that – for Tor's sake, we'd always tried to pretend we were all fine about Mum not being around, but it was times like this that it stung us pretty badly, too... Still, Tor was the important one, and we decided we'd all take turns spoiling him stupid over the weekend, starting with Linn today. Luckily, the clothes shop she works in on Saturdays was closed for the weekend while it was being redecorated, so she'd decided to take Tor to the Natural History Museum to coo over the dinosaur skeletons. To be honest, Linn was so uptight at the idea of Tor being unhappy that she might have taken the day off anyway. I think with Grandma being on holiday she saw herself as next in line for responsibility and sorting stuff out.

Since me and Rowan couldn't do anything useful to help, we were distracting ourselves by shopping. Shopping for – wait for it – belly-dancing stuff. (How did I let her talk me into it?)

"Ooh! Look at that! *That* would make a brilliant skirt!" Rowan sighed happily, pointing at a shop window brightly decorated in multi-coloured, gold-edged Indian silks.

I couldn't really make out which one she was pointing at, the display was crammed with so many prints and colours. Anyway, I didn't know why she was drooling. We'd already been in five identical sari shops along the length of Turnpike Lane and the only thing she'd found was that she had expensive taste. Every single bit of fabric she fell for ended up costing about twenty times more than any other bit of material on any other shelf in the entire shop. All we had bought so far was loads of thin, coloured metal bangles (for Rowan, to go with all the other thin, coloured metal bangles she already had), and a tinkly silver ankle chain (for me, though I still hadn't made up my mind whether I was going to give the class another chance or not).

"Come on..." I said firmly, steering Rowan past the latest window. "You said we could go for a burger while you had a think about what you wanted to buy, so let's go!"

"OK," shrugged Rowan, pretending that was fine by her, but sneaking a quick, longing look back at the window.

"What about this place?" I asked her, pointing to a small caff.

It wasn't exactly what you'd call trendy (it was more what you'd call scuzzy), and it definitely wasn't a great boy-spotting venue like McDonald's or Burger King round the corner on Wood Green High Street (there wasn't much to choose from between the two old geezers reading their papers and a bunch of fat-looking, builder-type blokes), but at least we'd get a table. At this time of the afternoon, the Saturday crowds were so bad on the High Street that we'd have had about as much chance of getting a seat in McD's or BK as I had of ever being Alfie's girlfriend – i.e. considerably less than zero. (Boo hoo.)

"Yeah, fine," Rowan nodded, pushing the door open and heading for the red vinyl window seat.

Once we got ourselves settled, we spotted the big board on the wall behind the counter, with the menu printed on it. As I was doing "eenie-meenie-miny-mo" between the burger with chips and the burger *without* chips (hey, I was trying to think of my jelly belly), I couldn't help but let my gaze slip down from the menu board to the two blokes serving behind the counter. They seemed to be mesmerized by the vision of Ro, and who could blame them? She might be worrying as much as the rest of us about Tor, but the worry certainly didn't stop her from dressing up in her usual eyeball-frying way. Today she had on a bright pink vest top, a cherry-red cardie, a swirly-patterned, turquoise and green knee-length skirt and last summer's yellow flip-flops with huge daisies on them.

After one of the men had come over to take our order – staring the whole time in awe-struck amazement at the flock of multi-coloured feathery clips perched all over her head – Rowan rested her chin on her hands and gazed at me.

"You know advice pages in magazines?" she began.

"Uh-huh," I nodded, taking my anklet out of the bag and running the chunky chain and bells through my fingers.

I didn't know where Rowan might be going with this conversation, but then I often don't know where Rowan's conversations are going. The internal workings of Ro's mind are like a magical mystery tour.

"They always say that when there's a problem, you should be honest with people."

"So?" I frowned at her.

"Well... Now that we know Tor's been upset about Mum, don't you think we should tell him the truth?" she asked, raising her arched eyebrows at me. "Y'know – that she left because she was depressed..."

"...and that we've no idea when she's coming back? Or *if* she's ever planning on coming back?" I finished her sentence for her, knowing that I sounded a bit harsh, but it was only 'cause the whole thing kind of stressed me out, if you want to know the truth.

Rowan bit her lip.

"It's just that he's only seven, Ro," I said, more gently. "I don't know if he can handle hearing big, scary stuff like that."

"But the advice pages say—"

I never did hear whatever else the advice pages said, 'cause at that moment we were interrupted by a sudden, loud banging on the window.

Both of us jumped – like practically everyone else in the café – expecting some kind of trouble. It was trouble all right – it was Kyra.

"Hiya!" she said loudly, breezing through the door as the blokes behind the counter visibly relaxed and put down their bread knives, now that they realized the commotion was caused by one thirteen-year-old girl and not a gang of roving football hooligans or something. "Fancy running into you! I was going to ring you later, Ally."

"Oh, yeah? What about?" I asked her, budging up so she could plonk herself down.

"I just wanted to see if you fancied going to the movies tonight," she said, squashing a white plastic bag on the table in front of her.

"Oh, yeah? What's on?"

"Some new thing with Matt Damon. Or is it

Jared Leto? I can't remember. Whatever. Fancy it?"

Kyra wasn't exactly selling the film very well, but I hadn't anything much planned – Dad was treating Tor to a bucket of Häagen Dazs and *Stuart Little* (a favourite vid for Tor – duh, *no* surprise), so I'd just planned on schlepping round to Sandie's.

"Yeah, OK," I shrugged. "So where've you been today?"

"Just been shopping round on the High Street. Look!"

Kyra said it so loud, I could sense the whole café joining in and noseying at whatever it was that she was pulling out of the plastic bag. By their expressions I didn't think the builders were that impressed by her tiny T-shirt with the words *Boys Suck! Girls Rule!* in silver lettering on the front. One of the old blokes narrowed his eyes to peer at it harder through his specs, then shook his head and looked confused. The other old bloke was just fast asleep over his newspaper.

"Nice!" Rowan nodded enthusiastically, fingering the lettering.

"So, what've you two been buying?" she asked, checking out the small paper bag on the table beside Rowan, and then clocking the anklet I'd been playing with. "What's this?"

"It's … it's an anklet," I answered, as I watched Kyra yank it from my hand.

She turned it this way and that, then shook it hard – *so* hard the tinkling of the tiny bells woke the snoozy old bloke up.

"Is this yours, Rowan?" she asked my sister.

It was pretty reasonable for her to suppose that something that fancy was Ro's. And actually, I'd really have liked Kyra to carry on thinking that since I didn't want her knowing…

"It's for belly dancing!" Rowan trilled innocently. "Ally got that and I got these!"

But Ro was wasting her time, spilling all her bangles out on to the formica table. Kyra had lost interest in Rowan's shopping immediately – now she was staring at me as though she'd just found out I was a Martian.

"*Belly* dancing?!" Kyra roared, aghast. "You two are going *belly* dancing?!"

Gee, thanks. Now every guy in the café was choking on his tea at this news. Their brains were probably scrambling as they tried to work out how the weird girl who was dressed like a tube of Smarties and the schoolkid in the baggy T-shirt and grey tracky bottoms could possibly, *feasibly* be belly dancers.

"Didn't Ally, er … tell you we've started going

to belly-dance classes?" said Rowan tentatively, as the truth slowly dawned on her.

No I flippin' *hadn't* told Kyra Davies. Did Rowan really think I fancied twenty-four-hour teasing over this? 'Cause knowing Kyra like I did, this was going to be the biggest, best mickey-taking experience of her life, without a shred of a doubt. I'd well and truly had it. I might as well switch schools, switch *boroughs* if I didn't want to get ribbed to death for ever after over this.

Or maybe not...

"You are *kidding*!" Kyra yelped, slapping her hands on the table so loudly that the sugar bowl jumped. "I've *always* wanted to do that! I saw this *amazing* dancer in a restaurant when we were in Turkey on holiday last year, and I thought 'yeah! I want to do that!' Oh, wow! I *have* to come with you! What night is it on?"

Kyra at belly-dance class. Now *why* was something telling me this might not be a good idea...?

"Where's Tor?" I asked Linn, as me and Rowan collapsed on to the sofa after our shopping trip.

I was curious to know because there was some kind of animal programme on the telly and there was no little brother sitting glued to it.

"He's gone next door to show that new vet bloke

a drawing he did of the dinosaur," said Linn, putting down her magazine now that we'd come in.

"Poor bloke," I smirked, sliding down the sofa and sticking my feet up on the coffee table, on either side of a purring cat that wasn't Colin. "Doesn't he realize that Michael's maybe only interested in animals that *aren't* extinct?"

Then I suddenly noticed how much my tum was sticking out (shouldn't have had those chips with my burger) and stopped smirking straight away.

"Listen, there's a problem with Tor," Linn announced, looking agitated.

"Like what?!" Rowan blinked at her.

"Like … I think there's more to this thing with Mum," Linn sighed.

"Why?" I frowned at her, feeling my heart sink like a big, old hunk of rock. I'd really *hoped* all that was sorted, after Dad having his little chat with him the night before.

"Well, today on the bus home, I tried to talk to him, y'know, about everything," Linn began. "I said to Tor that he shouldn't keep secrets, 'cause they can make you sad."

"You mean, not speaking to any of us about how much he was missing Mum?" Rowan asked her.

"Yeah, exactly," Linn nodded. "But then he said

the weirdest thing to me; he said sometimes it's better *not* to tell secrets, 'cause *telling* them can make you sad too."

"Huh?" Rowan scowled in confusion.

"Well," Linn continued, "*then* I asked him what he meant, and he wouldn't tell me. So I tried tickling it out of him."

"Smart move," I said approvingly, admiring her quick thinking.

Tickling had always been an approved method of torturing information out of people in our family.

"So – what did he say?" asked Ro, on the edge of the sofa by this point.

"He said," Linn sighed again, "that he knew something about Mum that he couldn't tell me – because it would make me too sad. And then he wouldn't say anything else; he just stared out the bus window. And I didn't feel like tickling him any more after that."

Uh-oh – it looked like we still didn't know *all* the secrets that were floating around inside our little brother's head...

Chapter 15

BILLY AND THE BELLY-FLIP

Going to the movies on a Saturday night: brilliant.
  Normally.

Going to the movies this particular Saturday
night? *Not* brilliant, for several reasons.

The first reason was Richie/Ricardo. When
me and Sandie mooched on up to meet Kyra at
the Muswell Hill Odeon, we didn't realize she'd
planned to include her big-headed boyfriend in
the invitation.

But there they both were, snogging like mad,
while other cinema-goers tutted or tittered their
way past them.

"Hi!" I said, on behalf of both myself and
Sandie.

Kyra and Richie/Ricardo were both too super-
glued to each other to notice us. Sandie pulled a
little "blee!" face at me and I tried again.

"Hi! Kyra! Yoo *hoo*!" I said, louder.

"Oh, hi!" Kyra grinned, coming up for air and
having the decency to look slightly flustered.

Richie/Ricardo on the other hand was doing this sort of Elvis sneer at me and Sandie and looking pretty pleased with himself, as if snogging his girlfriend in public was some major status symbol or something. Yeah, right. Everyone all around was *so* impressed, I *don't* think.

"All right, Richie?" I asked him, just to show that I had manners even if he didn't.

"Yuh-uh," he grunted, then turned and walked into the foyer.

You wouldn't think I'd helped the guy out a few weeks ago; helped him get back with Kyra when they'd split up (don't ask which time – there's been too many to count). He must have felt like that was a show of weakness or something, and now he was going to pretend it had never happened by only ever grunting at me.

Still, no matter how distant or conceited Richie/ Ricardo acted with me, the one thing I'd always have over him is the mental picture of him in my head wearing Billy's mum's lavender satin bra and knickers last Saturday night...

"Hey! I was telling Ricardo about belly-dancing classes!" Kyra beamed over her shoulder at me and Sandie as she and Mr Charmless stood in the ticket queue in front of us.

Urgh. Since I hadn't even told Chloe and my

other mates about going to belly dancing, I think it's a hundred and ninety-nine per cent safe to say that I didn't want Richie/Ricardo to know about it. And with good reason…

"Hur, hur, hur, hur!" he snickered, sounding like a five year old who'd just heard someone say a rude word.

"It's not foxy or anything!" I burst out, trying to defend myself.

Well, when *I* did it, it certainly wasn't foxy, unless you think someone dancing like a cross between a constipated duck and a plank of wood is foxy. (Mind you, a lot of the women who'd been going for ages – even the ones with really big jelly bellies – looked quite foxy and cool doing all the moves the way they're meant to be done.)

But I was wasting my time, trying to explain anything to Richie/Ricardo.

"Hur, hur, hur, hur!" he snickered some more.

And he *kept* snickering to himself, all the way till we got our seats, right up at the back of the cinema.

"…I wonder what I'll wear to class on Tuesday…" Kyra wittered away loudly while the ads were on. "What does everyone else wear, Ally?"

"Not much! Hur, hur, hur!" sniggered Richie/Ricardo.

I suddenly wished someone had invented the technology to put ejector buttons on seats. Then when anyone at the cinema ate popcorn with their mouths open, or talked too loudly during the film, or just happened to be Richie/Ricardo, they could simply be disposed of with one quick shove of that magic button.

"Ignore him," I heard Sandie whisper to me.

She'd sensibly wangled it, I noticed, to be sitting as far away from Richie/Ricardo as she could, with me and Kyra in-between them both. I wished *I'd* thought of that. In fact, I wished we hadn't come at all. I wish me and Sandie had carried on hanging out in her bedroom (even with those mad painted daisies looming down on us from the walls), where we'd been discussing life, the universe and Tor, of course. Instead, we'd come to see a movie we didn't even know would be any good and were having to endure the torture of listening to Richie/ Ricardo hur-hurring, and him and Kyra play tonsil tennis (more of which was bound to happen when the film started).

"Hey, Kyra – you'll never guess!" said Sandie, changing the conversation away from the dodgy area of belly dancing once the lights came on between the ads and the movie. "Mum got me to put my hand on her stomach today and I felt the baby kicking!"

"Did you!" Kyra gasped, marvelling at the alien weirdness of Sandie's future brother or sister making contact with the outside world.

As Sandie babbled away, describing what it felt like, I could see Richie/Ricardo glaze over with boredom. Then suddenly, he perked up – pointing over the crowded rows of seats at the couple making their way to some empty places right at the front.

"Hey, look!" he cried. "It's Billy! Hold on, I'll give him a shou—"

In a millionth of a nano-second, I clocked who Billy was with – it was Anita, the Sports Shop Girl. And instantly, I stretched past Kyra and slapped my hand over Richie/Ricardo's big mouth.

"Don't you dare!" I hissed. "He's on a date! Don't shout – you'll just *mortify* him!"

Richie/Ricardo looked at me with his long-lashed eyes like I was a freak, then shrugged.

"Ohhkaahh," the word came muffled through my fingers.

It seemed safe; I let go.

"Yeah? Billy's on a date? Who with?" Kyra asked, doing an excellent giraffe impression as she stretched her neck up to have a nosey.

"Just a girl. It's no big deal."

Of course it was a big deal – for Billy. I couldn't

imagine how nervous he must be feeling. He was probably sitting down there now hyperventilating. And he'd hyperventilate even more if Richie/Ricardo went yelling at him in front of a couple of hundred people.

"Jeez!" he muttered. "Billy said he was taking some bird out sometime—"

"Bird?" Kyra hauled him up.

"—uh, girl – whatever," Richie/Ricardo shrugged. "But he never let on when he was going out with her, or that she was such a total *babe*..."

Oops. Richie/Ricardo seemed to have temporarily forgotten that his girlfriend was sitting right next to him. Well, maybe they wouldn't be snogging their way through the movie *after* all.

And we'd soon see – the lights were going down now. I could hardly make out Billy's baseball-cap-free head any more...

"Are you OK?" Sandie whispered, holding out her Butterkist to me, as the credits rolled.

"Yeah!" I nodded, while waving no to the Butterkist on account of my jelly belly.

But the funny thing was, I *wasn't* all right, and that wasn't because of the worry about Tor and his secret, and it wasn't 'cause I was stuck in the company of a dork like Richie/Ricardo. It was because ... because I was *hurt*, if you want to know.

142

I know it sounds weird, but I was feeling pretty gutted that Billy – after me asking Anita out for him and everything – hadn't bothered to phone me and tell me that they'd arranged their date for tonight. When had he called her? Thursday night, after I'd given him her phone number? Or last night? Or had he gone into the shop and planned it with her today? Whenever, he must have been *so* excited, yet he hadn't thought, "I know, I'll phone Ally and tell her!" like he normally would about anything big going on with him. It was really stupid I know, but I almost felt like I'd been *dumped*.

And then it got weirder. I couldn't concentrate on the film – my mind kept meandering off – until this one scene where there was a close-up of the hero leaning forward and looking into the heroine's eyes, and you just *knew* that the Big Kiss was about one second away. Right then, I felt this twisty, belly-flip thing happen – and all because I'd suddenly, *bizarrely*, imagined Billy doing the same thing; leaning forward to kiss Anita…

God! I yelped in my head, feeling this huge shudder quake its way down my spine. *Why does the thought of Billy and Anita snogging freak me out so much?*

It wasn't like I'd ever wanted to *be* there – kissing Billy, I mean. Oh, *no*. It would just be too

143

mad, imagining him with his nice but goofy face, staring into my eyes, all serious for once, and then blinking shyly, and coming closer and closer, his lips zeroing in on mine, until—

"Coke?" whispered Sandie, holding a bucket with a straw under my nose.

"No!" I squeaked, feeling almost like I might faint, or barf, or both...

"Billy and that bird must have gone out another exit," said Richie/Ricardo, gazing around the foyer at the rapidly thinning crowds spilling out of the Screen 1 doors.

What does *he sound like, with all this "bird" business?* I thought, shooting him a narrow-eyed, sideways glance. He seemed to be forgetting that he was a thirteen-year-old boy from a middle-class street in Muswell Hill, not a fifty-year-old gangster...

Anyway, the last thing I wanted was to see Billy and his "bird", after all the mental things that had been boinging about in my brain during the movie. All I wanted to do was get out of here, get home and get those stupid thoughts out of my head. But I couldn't shoot off yet – Sandie and Kyra were both still in the loo, leaving me on my own (arrrghh!) with Richie/Ricardo.

"So…" he grunted, giving up scanning for Billy, and suddenly looking just as uncomfortable as I was that we were alone together.

"So…" I repeated, trying frantically to think of something, *anything*, to say to him.

"So … the other day at school—"

Wow, Richie/Ricardo was attempting to make conversation. Ten out of ten for effort!

"—Billy was telling us – hur, hur! – that a couple of poofs have moved in next door to you!"

And minus a *trillion* points for saying something really obnoxious.

I tell you, if I'd still been sitting on my chair, I'd have fallen off it. I was shocked: for one thing, it had never occurred to me that Michael and his lodger might be anything other than, well … Michael and his lodger. When I thought about it, then yeah, it might be true – maybe they *were* gay (maybe that's why Grandma had gone a bit "hmm…" when she first heard about them). But why had Billy been gossiping about it to his mates like it was something seedy and snigger-worthy?

To think, ten minutes ago, I'd almost imagined *kissing* Billy – now I couldn't imagine why he was ever my friend in the first place…

145

Chapter 16

THE HEALING POWER OF BISCUITS...

One of my trainers was on the loose somewhere in the house.

"This isn't something to do with you, is it?" I asked Winslet, who looked me straight in the eye and said nothing. (Huh, that's dogs for you – no help at all.)

I was on my hands and knees checking under the sofa – with Rolf and Winslet helping, just to hurry me so we could get out for our Sunday morning walk – when I heard the phone ring in the hall.

Rolf and Winslet stopped snuffling under the sofa, stared off in the direction of the phone, and then back at me.

"OK, OK! I'll get it!" I huffed at them, scrambling up on to my feet. "Though I don't know why no one else can..."

Actually no one else could because they were either out (Rowan had – amazingly! – got up early and taken Tor swimming), in the shower (Dad – I could hear him yodelling from here) or working

(Linn – helping put the clothes shop back together again now that the painters had done their thing).

"Hello?"

"Hey, guess what?" said Kyra's voice.

"What?"

"I've chucked Ricardo."

"Good," I said, sounding probably a little bit too chuffed. "Why?"

"He was just bugging me last night," Kyra yawned. "You should have heard him after you and Sandie left – he kept going *on* and *on* and *on* about how cute Billy's new girlfriend was."

Billy... I was on my way to meet him soon, as usual, even though it felt pretty *un*usual after everything I'd thought, seen and heard last night.

"So how are you feeling?" I asked her, brushing aside how weird I felt. "Are you all right about chucking him?"

"Sure. Anyway, I thought I'd give that thing of yours a go."

"What thing?" I frowned.

"That just-being-friends-with-boys thing," Kyra explained. "I'm bored of having boyfriends – it's a total pain."

That was funny; just when I was reluctantly swinging round more to *her* way of thinking – that it was impossible to be friends with boys – there was Kyra, swinging around to *mine*.

"Listen, Kyra – I've got to go," I told her, as Winslet and Rolf sat on my feet staring up at me soulfully with their leads in their mouths. "I'll call you back later, OK?"

But two seconds after I put the phone down, it rang again.

"Kyra?" I asked, thinking she'd forgotten something.

"Huh?" mumbled Billy.

"Billy? I thought you were Kyra!" I explained badly, irritated with myself for getting all kerfuffled at the sound of his voice.

"Hi, Ally," he said, sounding pretty sheepish himself.

"What's up?" I asked him. "I was just on my way to meet you…"

"Aw, listen – I can't make it today. I'm … well, I'm meeting Anita. We're going to feed the ducks on the boating pond…"

And there I was – dumped. Though I shouldn't have *really* been bothered since I was still technically annoyed with Billy (even if he didn't know it).

"Oh?" was all I managed to say.

"Yeah! And, hey Ally! Guess what? I went out

with Anita last night and it was *really* good!" he burbled.

"Oh, yeah?"

For a second, I wondered if I should interrupt and tell Billy that I saw him and Anita on their date, but he kept wittering on so much that I couldn't get a word in edgeways.

"Uh-huh – brilliant, isn't it?!" he beamed down the phone, ignoring the flatness of my voice and assuming that I was like, *amazingly* excited for him.

"So, I met her from her work, and we went for chips, and then we went to see that new Matt Damon movie at Muswell Hill Odeon—"

As Billy blabbered, Dad thumped downstairs in his dressing gown, giving my hair a ruffle as he passed on his way to the kitchen.

"—and she's really cool and everything. 'Cause she thought the film was rubbish, same as me, and she supports Arsenal, so that's OK. Oh, and she likes mayonnaise as well as tomato sauce on chips too – like I do!"

Billy sounded so happy, you'd think he'd just heard he'd won a lifetime's supply of Toblerone or something.

"And I really think she likes me, even though she's fourteen, and she didn't make me feel like a kid at all – well, not much. And … and … are you still there, Ally?

"Yeah," I nodded, not that he could see me.

"Uh … you're pretty quiet."

"It's just that … I've got to go. Dad wants me for something," I fibbed, as a tiny twitch started under my eye.

"OK, see you…" Billy's voice trailed off as I put the receiver down.

You know something? I had no idea why, but my head was totally messed up. No – it had gone beyond messed up: it had turned to *mush*. In fact my head was so mushy that it was a miracle that Dad managed to recognize me when I slobbed through to the kitchen, with two disappointed dogs trailing after me.

I needed something to cheer me up, and I had a feeling that something might be hiding in the biscuit tin.

"Diving into the biscuits at this time in the morning? It *must* be bad," Dad grinned at me, as he poured himself a cup of tea.

I flopped down on one of the kitchen chairs with an "I-dunno" shrug.

"Here – give me one of those," he said, leaning over for a HobNob, "I'm feeling a bit 'shruggy' myself today."

"How come?" I asked him, while breaking my KitKat into three pieces. (One bit for me, one bit for Rolf, one bit for Winslet...)

"Oh, I just wish I was a bit better at getting Tor to talk to me," he sighed, sitting down opposite me. "Maybe I should do a Mrs Doubtfire and dress up as your gran – she always seems to know what's going on with him."

The thought of my tall, skinny dad wearing my small, neat Grandma's sensible twinsets and slacks made me grin a chocolatey grin.

"Well, she didn't know about *this* stuff – about him missing Mum and everything," I pointed out, covering my KitKat-covered teeth with my hand.

"Maybe not..." Dad mused. "Still, I'll be glad when she gets back next Saturday and can maybe get to the bottom of this secret business that's bothering him."

Suddenly – and for the very first time ever – I thought of Mum and got kind of cross. OK, so she was always good at sending us letters and cards and photos, but I wished just once in a while she could go crazy and use that amazing new technological invention they call the Telephone. Maybe Tor wouldn't miss her so much if he could *talk* to her now and then. And the same goes for me too...

"But anyway, Ally Pally," said Dad, slapping a breezy smile on his face. "What's up with you? And why aren't you dragging these beasts round the park right now?"

That's what the "beasts" were wondering too. They'd put down their leads for a second while I tried to bribe them with KitKat, but they'd both grabbed them up again and were sitting on either side of me gazing at me hopefully.

"That's the problem – the park ... well, Billy," I mumbled, making probably zero sense.

"What? Have you fallen out with him?" asked Dad, helping himself to another HobNob.

"Something like that..." I sighed. "Well, no – not really. It's just that he's been doing lots of dumb stuff lately."

I didn't think I could handle gabbing on about the whole Billy and Anita thing and how bizarre it made me feel. Instead, I decided I'd just stick with the business of Billy being a berk.

"Dumb stuff? Like what?" asked Dad.

"Like showing off in front of his mates," I explained, thinking of the way he played down his date with Anita when we'd met Hassan and Steven in the park on Thursday. "And he sometimes acts different towards me when he's with his friends, too."

"Right..." Dad nodded, scratching his newly shaved chin thoughtfully.

"And he said something really crummy," I continued. "He told his mate that we had 'poofs' living next door to us. That's not nice, is it?"

"No, it isn't, and you should tell him that," said Dad. "But Billy's a good lad – I'm sure he didn't mean it nastily. He must have just blurted it out to the boys to try and sound funny or something, and it came out tactless instead."

"But why do boys do that?" I tried to understand. "Why do they act all goofy and do stupid things when they're with their mates? I mean, you never did that, did you?"

"Course I did!" Dad laughed, surprising me. "It can be tough as a lad when you're growing up, you know – you're trying to fit in with your friends all the time and be part of the gang, and sometimes you get it wrong. Don't be too hard on Billy, love – remember, you girls have it easier 'cause you can talk to each other about feelings and stuff, and boys don't really do that."

Wow, I hadn't thought of it that way, but I guessed it tied in with what Rowan had said about boys not showing their emotions too well. Maybe I should feel sorry for Billy, then, and not get so bugged by his berkiness.

"So is that it? Is that all that's been bothering you about him?" asked Dad.

I was about to lie and say yes, when I suddenly realized – duh! – Dad might be the very person to answer the question that had been loitering at the back (and sometimes the front) of my mind this last week or so.

After all, he had been a boy, once upon a time, hadn't he?

"Actually, Dad," I began, thinking of the very words Kyra had used that day we'd been sitting up by Alexandra Palace, "do you think boys and girls can really be friends? Or does fancying each other get in the way?"

"Why?" he asked, his eyes twinkling at me. "Has something happened with you and Billy?"

"No!" I yelped. "It's just that … well … he's started going out with this girl, and it's made me feel … kind of *funny*."

"Funny, ha-ha?" he teased me. "Or funny, jealous?"

"Um, jealous, I suppose," I replied reluctantly.

"Yeah, Ally, but are you jealous because *you* want to be going out with him instead of her, or because your friend is hanging out with someone else instead of you?"

My mushy head starting whirling as I thought

that over. The thing was, I wasn't jealous *jealous*, like *I* wanted to hold his hand or anything like that. No, I was jealous 'cause my best (boy) friend had found a new girl to hang out with. A new girl who he liked more than *me*. I mean, I don't like football (and I hate mayonnaise on chips), so it was obvious that he was going to like this cooler, older girl more than me. Soon, I'd never get to hang out with Billy, would I? He'd think meeting up on Sundays to walk dogs was just for kids or something...

And *that*'s what was wrong. Talking it out with Dad had somehow sorted it out for me: I didn't fancy Billy at all, not one bit – even though I'd run through thoughts of kissing him in my head, just to see what that felt like (and it felt as nuts as snogging *Rolf*). Nope, it wasn't a boy/girl thing: I was just jealous of losing my friend, the same way Sandie had been jealous not so long ago when she thought me and Kyra were buddying up and leaving her out.

"I don't fancy him – I'm just scared he'll like her more than me!" I announced.

"There you go then!" said Dad. "There's the mystery solved. And you don't have to feel envious of this girl – maybe Billy's got a crush on her, but *you're* his friend, and that's two separate things!"

This was brilliant – I felt like someone had

turned a tap on in my head and washed all the mush away. It was simple – berk or not, Billy was my mate, and that was all there was to it.

I was so happy, I decided to celebrate with another biscuit...

Chapter 17

SHIMMIES, SNIGGERS AND I-SPY...

"That's not bad, Ally," said Glittery Gloria, walking towards me in a haze of twinkly, tinkling bits. "But let's see more of a pelvic tilt going on there. Come on – *push* the pelvis forward! And *push* – that's it!"

I didn't know whether I was practising a) a dance move, or b) for giving birth at a future date. All I *did* know was that I had a crushing pain in my chest from trying very, *very* hard not to burst out laughing. And it was all that Kyra Davies's fault...

It had been a bad idea to let her come along to belly-dance class. Maybe Kyra wanted to be a belly dancer, but she sure didn't want to bother herself with the boring bit of learning *how* to do it. Every time we practised a hip lift or a hip drop, Kyra (who wasn't acting exactly heartbroken about her recent break-up) would let out a loud "Fnar!!" or "Pffff!" of a snigger and mutter stuff like "She's *got* to be joking!"

Then when Gloria had shouted "Shimmy,

ladies!" and Kyra saw everyone in the room suddenly start shaking their clinking, coin-covered bums at high speed ... well, she lost it completely. And you *know* how contagious giggles are. Even though I wanted to strangle Kyra and tell her to grow up, I wouldn't have been able to open my mouth to say anything in case I burst into giggles too. Which made me want to strangle her even *more*.

Von and Rowan, I'd noticed, had decided that the best thing to do with Kyra was to pretend they didn't know her – or me. They'd started off the lesson standing at the back of the room, where we'd been the week before, but every time I stopped concentrating on my pelvis or trying not to laugh, I'd check their whereabouts and see them moving further and further to the front.

They blended in pretty well with the other women now, I noticed. Rowan and Von both had more bright jewellery on, and had tied shawl-type things around their hips to look like everyone else's fancy coin hip belts. I was still in my running trousers and vest – with the addition, of course, of my bell-covered anklet. Not that you could see it under my trousers, but you *could* just hear it, tinkling out of time as I constantly got the beat wrong.

"OK, ladies! And just have a rest for a moment!" crooned Gloria, thankfully letting go of my pelvis as the jingly track faded out.

"This is *mad*!" Kyra hissed in my ear. "Could you imagine people ever seeing us *doing* this stuff?!"

"Shush, Kyra!" I hissed back, trying to sound grumpy and *desperately* trying not to catch her eye in case she set me off.

"Now then, ladies, while you catch your breath, I'd just like to remind you about the performance we're going to give at the church fête on Saturday," Gloria began, as she set about changing the tape in her machine.

I blanked out at that point, letting her chatter on about times and details of the rehearsal for the benefit of all the women who'd be taking part in it. Instead, I ended up staring at the ghastly, psychedelic-patterned curtains that were pulled closed all around the room and idly wondering if the vicar of this church was a big fan of the seventies or something, to have chosen them. Maybe he did his Sunday sermons in big, flappy flares and platform shoes. Maybe he had a lava lamp on the pulpit. Well, it could give really little kids something to look at during the service, 'cause little toddlers and everything, they can get twitchy and bored sitting still so long when they don't really understand what's going on...

I was still lost in this idea of the grooviest church in Crouch End when my mind was dragged back to reality with ten terrifying words.

"We'd love to have you new girls in the show."

Whaaaaaaaaaaaaat? I screamed silently in my head, as Gloria beamed at me, Rowan, Von – and even Kyra.

"Wouldn't we, ladies?" Gloria smiled a the rest of the class. "You newies are all doing *so* well!"

As all the women turned and clapped and grinned encouragingly at us, my heart plummeted down the lift shaft of my body and landed with a plop at my feet. Rowan and Von, I noticed, were exchanging excited glances.

Oh, help...

"But we don't know enough!" I heard Rowan say.

Hurrah! Someone was getting real here!

"Ah, but we can just get you girls in the background, doing some simple hip drops while we do the main routine at the front!" Gloria announced casually. "If we have you holding up some lovely veils, then it'll look very effective!"

Rowan turned and chucked me a quick glance over her shoulder, all nervous and wide-eyed.

I *hoped* my expression read "No – please, no! Get us out of this, Rowan, and get us out of this NOW!", but Rowan seemed to think it said, "Yes – please say yes! Let's embarrass ourselves in front of a whole hall full of people and never be able to walk through Crouch End without a paper bag over our heads ever again!"

"What do you say, girls?" Gloria asked, tossing her jet-black hair back over one tanned shoulder.

"Brilliant! We'll do it!" Rowan giggled. "Won't we, Von? Won't we, Ally?"

Von was nodding so much her head was in danger of falling off. I just wished mine *would* fall off so I could get out of this stupid situation I'd got myself into.

Kyra, meanwhile, was shaking so much with the giggles that she looked like she was doing an all-over body shimmy.

Could this get any worse?

"OK, ladies," Gloria boomed over the opening ripples of music starting up on the next tape. "Let's really give those hip thrusts a work out here. Listen to those drums, Ally, and get that pelvis tilting!"

Oh, yes, it could get worse. And it wasn't because I was sure my dancing technique had all the grace of a Teletubby crossed with a rhinoceros, or because Kyra had now gone beyond stifling her giggles and was honking like a goose.

It was because of the curtains. Everything was *much* worse because right there, where two of the hideous curtains didn't *quite* meet were four sniggering faces ogling in at us all.

And I'll give you three guesses who they were.

Actually, I won't bother.

Let's just say Billy and his stupid mates were dead meat.

And let's just say all those good vibes I'd had about Billy after the chat with Dad on Sunday – well, they were *history*...

Chapter 18

THE DANGERS OF DOODLING...

Of course, the lads disappeared pretty quickly when Gloria stomped over and pulled the curtains tightly shut. Or maybe it was the way she roared at them through the church-hall window, frightening them off with her glittery bits and her long, black hair and kohl-dark eyes.

"They must have thought she was some exotic, gypsy witch who was about to turn them into newts or something," said Rowan, taking the mug of coffee I was holding out to her.

It was twenty minutes since our class had disastrously finished, and me, Rowan and Kyra had come back to our house for a moan about the rubbishness of boys. Or at least the rubbishness of boys called Billy Stevenson and his stupid bunch of morons. Sorry, *mates*. Actually, no – I got it right the first time.

"Being turned into newts is too good for them," I sighed, passing another mug to Kyra and setting my own mug down on our kitchen table. "She should turn them into *plankton*."

"Ooh, don't let Tor hear you saying that!" grinned Linn, who was hovering around the kitchen, enjoying listening in to our grumbling session. "Plankton are living creatures who don't deserve to be slagged off in any way!"

(Anti-animal phrases like "You're a disgusting pig!", "What a *dog*!" and "Silly cow!" are a definite no-no in our house, thanks to our resident Animal Standards Officer, Mr Tor Love.)

"Well, she should just turn them into big, steamy piles of horse poo," I muttered childishly, wishing immediately that I'd tried to come out with something a bit smarter.

But I was burning up too much with shame to think of anything smarter. Billy and his morons hadn't just embarrassed *me* with their gawping session at the church hall – they'd embarrassed Kyra, Rowan, Von, and all the other girls and women in the class. How could Billy do that to me, when he was my friend? (Supposedly.)

Glittery Gloria had laughed it off, but I couldn't. Von certainly wasn't laughing, and she doesn't take much notice of me at the best of times, so this particular outrage wasn't exactly going to make her warm to me. She'd disappeared off home straight after class, giving me a ferociously disapproving look as she went. Rowan tried to convince me that it hadn't been disapproving – that Von always looks like that, but while I sort of know that's true, I couldn't shake off how truly mortified I felt.

"Don't be so disgusting, Ally," Linn frowned at me, after my steamy-poo comment.

She's funny, Linn – there she was telling me off in her best, bossy, big-sister way, but at the same time she was very kindly wafting the biscuit tin under my nose to try and cheer me up.

I knew it wouldn't help but I took a Ginger Nut anyway, just to be polite.

"God!" Kyra announced, slapping her hands on the table. "I am *so* finished with Ricardo!"

I noticed that Rowan and Linn looked vaguely impressed by Kyra's dramatic-sounding gesture. Not that I was.

"But Kyra, you already finished with him!" I pointed out.

"Yes, but this is *it*!" she nodded determinedly. "It was bad enough when I saw him wearing Billy's mother's knickers on his head, and drooling over that girl when we were out on Saturday, but when I saw him tonight, peeking in through the curtains and giggling, I thought *urgh*! I mean, it's the sort of thing a little kid does! *I'm* not going out with someone who acts like he's a goofy five year old!"

For a second I felt quite pleased. I'd always thought of Richie/Ricardo as a big-headed git with all the personality of a cardboard box, and if Kyra had finally decided to chuck him, I for one would be very chuffed. But then I got real: no matter how much he'd embarrassed her tonight or whenever, she'd probably forget her huff by the end of the week and be back snogging him by Saturday.

"How did the boys know about the class anyway?" Rowan suddenly asked.

"It's my fault," Kyra shrugged. "I told Ricardo about it, before I realized he was such a *loser*..."

"Yeah, but Billy was with them. Why didn't he stop them?" I chipped in miserably. "It was *so* awful..."

"Well, look, don't let it bug you *too* much, Ally," Rowan very sweetly tried to reassure me. "I mean, it wasn't like they saw us *nude* or anything. They just saw us doing a dance routine, that's all."

It was nice of her to try, but that's exactly why it was so awful. The idea of Billy, Hassan, Steven and Richie/Ricardo catching sight of us all hip thrusting made me feel positively ill...

I took another bite of Ginger Nut to try and keep the sick feeling at bay.

"You could always get them back," Linn grinned, putting the lid back on the tin after I went to help myself to a medicinal Jaffa Cake.

"How?" I asked, vaguely aware of the doorbell and Dad shouting "I'll get it!" in the background.

"Well, you know they do their football practice by the cricket pitch in Ally Pally," she shrugged. "So why don't you all go to the pavilion and sneak in on them when they're in the changing rooms?"

"Because they'd probably *love* it," Kyra pointed out dryly. "Them *and* the rest of the footie team!"

"Um, Ally?" we heard Dad interrupt from the kitchen doorway. "Friend to see you!"

I could have sued Dad under the Trades Descriptions Act for calling Billy a "friend" right then.

"Hey, it's Tom!" Kyra turned and greeted him sarcastically.

"Huh?" Billy mumbled, creasing his forehead in puzzled lines.

"Tom. As in Peeping Tom. That's what you are, isn't it?" Kyra said bluntly. "And where's the rest of the Peeping Toms? Or are they away sneaking a look in someone else's window?"

Having a mouthy friend like Kyra did have its benefits sometimes. Specially since I was so mad at Billy that I couldn't trust my mouth to blabber the words I wanted to say in the right order. And anyway, the *Boys Suck! Girls Rule!* T-shirt she had on said it all, really.

"Look, I just came round to say … well … sorry," Billy mumbled, glancing around the table at us all (even Linn, who hadn't got anything to do with anything), then gawped down at the floor.

You know how Kyra said Richie/Ricardo looked about five when he was peering through the windows on his tippy-toes? Well, that's about how old Billy looked right now, scuffing one toe of his Reeboks on the kitchen floor and pulling awkwardly at the hem of his T-shirt with his thumbs.

There was silence for a second, then I realized that everyone was waiting for *me* to say something.

"You…" I finally began angrily, struggling for the right words. "You…"

"I know! And I'm really sorry!" Billy said hurriedly, fixing me with this soppy, big sorrowful look and coming to sit down in the chair next to me at the table.

Unluckily for Billy, it growled. He'd yanked at the chair that Fluffy was sitting snoozing on, and she wasn't too thrilled. Instantly, Billy shoved the chair back under the table and went round to the spare chair next to Linn.

"Biscuit?" said Linn, pushing the tin towards him.

I shot her a murderous look for being such a traitor.

"No, it's OK," Billy shook his head.

Now that he was sitting down, I could make out two beads of sweat trickling down his forehead, from the rim of his sand-coloured NYC baseball cap.

"Honest, I'm really sorry," he continued. "We were at Hassan's, right round the corner from the church, and once Hassan had done his homework and we'd all copied it off him –"

The four of us girls rolled our eyes at that – not that Billy noticed.

"– we were really bored. And then Richie remembered you said stuff about that class, and we just thought it would be a laugh to come round and sneak a look at what you were doing…"

"What – as much of a laugh as wearing your mum's bra on your head?" Kyra blinked at him coolly.

Billy winced at that little barb and shrugged.

"OK, I know I should have maybe talked the lads out of it, but they kept saying it would be fun!" Billy defended himself pathetically.

"Nice one, Billy," I nodded at him. "You've just proved what I've started to think lately."

"What?" he frowned, knowing that whatever

I was about to say probably *wasn't* going to be a compliment.

"That boys are rubbish."

(By the way, I wasn't including Alfie in this. Beautiful love-gods definitely qualified for the Boys Are Rubbish get-out clause.)

"Are not!" Billy protested.

"Are too!" I replied.

"Boys are brilliant!" Billy blurted out, widening his eyes as much as he was pursing his lips.

"Yeah? Well, prove it!" I challenged him. "*We'll* all write a list of reasons why boys are rubbish, and *you* can write a list of why boys are brilliant!"

"That'll be a pretty short list," Kyra snorted.

"Fine! Let's do it!" Billy agreed hotly, while ignoring Kyra's comment and my sisters' amused grins.

"Fine! I'll get some paper!" I announced, standing up and screeching my chair away from me.

After a half-second glance around the paper-free kitchen, I suddenly thought of my schoolbag, flopped outside on the hall floor under the coat rack. I stormed out to it, lifted Rolf's head off it without waking him, grabbed my ring binder and stomped back into the kitchen.

"Right, we get five minutes each to come up with a list, OK?" I told Billy, clattering the binder and a couple of pens on to the table.

I was starting to enjoy this. I'm not a mean person, but after what he'd put me through tonight, it was quite fun seeing Billy look so uncomfortable, faced with the might of four of us against one of him in this list-making challenge. And before Kyra and my sisters even started making suggestions, I knew I would streak ahead with plenty of my own. And top of the "Why Boys Are Rubbish" list would be "1) Do Dumb Things Without Thinking".

But uh-oh – right then *I* did a Very Dumb Thing Without Thinking. Oh dear…

There, in front of everyone, I flipped the binder open at the back – where there was plenty of spare paper to tear out – and practically *died* on the spot.

It wasn't just the fact that there were silly, dippy doodles of hearts and flowers all over the page. It was more the fact that all the hearts and flowers were surrounding about a thousand scribblings of one word. OK, one *name*. Guess which one.

"Alfie? 'I love *Alfie*'?" Billy roared at a million decibels, as soon as his eyes strayed on to the page.

(Did everyone in the entire street catch what he'd just said, I wondered?)

The second after Billy came out with that little

bombshell felt like the longest, no, make that the *looooonnnnggggeeessssttttttt* second in my life. The particular page that I'd opened my binder at had a tear in it, from when me, Kyra and Sandie had sat up Ally Pally playing the destiny game, a couple of weeks back. And I'd completely forgotten about it.

I couldn't speak. I couldn't move. I didn't dare look at my sisters – especially Linn – to see their reaction. I'd just shrivel up and *evaporate* if my secret was so horribly *out*.

"Oi!" I suddenly heard Kyra say, and saw her skinny, light brown arm shoot across the table and yank the page out, lightning fast.

Scrunching the paper up and shoving it in her pocket, Kyra shot me a hurt look. I was totally confused, as well as in shock. Part of my brain felt like it had *melted*.

"Thanks very much, Ally!" Kyra snapped at me. "You promised you'd get rid of that, so no one saw what I'd been writing!"

I was lost – I hadn't a clue what she was on about, I was so frozen with horror. But the way Kyra was staring at me, and something about the tiny, telltale twitch in her face stopped me from saying, "Huh...?"

"So now everyone knows I fancy your friend

Alfie," Kyra sighed theatrically, turning to face Linn. "God, I'm so embarrassed!"

"*My* Alfie?" Linn laughed incredulously. "Do you?"

"Yeah," Kyra sighed again. "You don't mind, do you, Linn? It's just that he's *so* mature. Not like *some* people and their mates..."

That last bit was aimed at Billy, of course. And Richie/Ricardo too, even if he wasn't there to get the benefit of it.

"Why should I mind?" smiled Linn. "It's a free country! You can fancy who you want!"

Kyra was my hero. And a very *fast* hero. Not only had she stepped in and saved my skin by pretending that *she'd* done the doodling, but she'd also pulled the page out so quickly that no one had the chance to recognize my writing.

Wow, I could have given Kyra a big, wet, soggy kiss thank-you right then, if that wasn't totally weird. And I could have slapped Billy with a big, wet, soggy fish for being so spectacularly loud and tactless.

What was I saying about boys being rubbish...?

Chapter 19

THE JELLY-BELLY JIGGLE

OK. It was Saturday morning, and after a couple of weeks' worth of intensive worrying (my speciality), there were a couple of things I now knew I *didn't* have to worry about.

Those were...

1) Having any kind of crush on Billy. I'd sorted that one out in my head, no problem.

2) Despite Billy acting the total muppet on Tuesday night (twice), at least my secret crush on Alfie was safe, thanks to Kyra's brilliant efforts. (Give that girl a gold star.)

Of course, the *flip*side of that was the things that I *did* have to worry about on this cloudy Saturday morning.

And *those* were...

1) I had to leave in ten minutes to go to a rehearsal for this dopey belly-dancing display at the church fête this afternoon.

2) I really, *really* didn't want to do this dopey belly-dancing display thing, but I knew Rowan

would be crushed at me letting her down if I didn't turn up.

3) But I still really, *really* didn't want to do it.

4) And because I really, *really* didn't want to do it, I hadn't done anything about sorting out a "costume" – i.e. a floaty skirt, a cropped top, a scarf for my hips, a paper bag for my head, etc.

5) Since I had to go to this stupid rehearsal, I didn't have time to go to the pet shop with Tor as usual, and this presented another problem. It wasn't that the hamsters would have to go without clean bedding for a while or that Stanley the goldfish wouldn't get the new underwater bush that Tor had promised him, it was just that it meant Tor couldn't pick the brains of the pet-shop owner about the weird lump on Stanley's side that was getting so big he was in danger of toppling over. Well, as much as you *can* topple over in water.

6) *Because* Tor hadn't been able to talk to the pet-shop owner, he'd decided to go next door and speak to Michael the Vet, his New Best Friend. I tried to explain that Michael might not be up yet or might be working, and Tor seemed to accept that, but as soon I'd gone into the living room in search of my trainer (yep, missing in action again), I saw a blur of small boy and goldfish bowl whisk past me in the hall and out of the front door.

Now I had exactly nine minutes to chase Rowan out of the shower (she's seriously bad at getting up early on weekend mornings), find something skirty to wear for the belly-dancing performance (nothing like leaving things till the last minute), and drag Tor away from No. 26 before our poor new neighbour regretted ever moving next door to us. And to do that, I'd have to find my other trainer – i.e. I'd have to find out where Winslet was first…

"Winslet! Winslet! Here, girl! Good dog!" I called out, tying the laces of the one trainer I'd found by the phone table in the hall.

Four faces appeared out of doorways and down the stairwell, all of them responding to my call and looking at me quizzically. Pity none of them was Winslet. Or a girl. Or a dog, even.

"Sorry, guys! It's nothing you can help me with!" I said to four cats that weren't Colin, who'd sleepily uncurled themselves and come noseying at what the commotion was all about.

"Hi!" called out a voice behind me, as I heard the front door creaking open.

Sadly it wasn't Winslet, who'd magically learnt to speak and wanted to return my trainer instantly. It was Billy.

"It was already open," he explained, pointing at the door.

"Uh-huh – Tor must have left it open," I muttered, rummaging under the schoolbags in the hall in case they were hiding my trainer.

"Is he here?" Billy asked nervously, darting his eyes around like he was searching for signs of a poltergeist.

"Not right this second – he's next door, with our new *neighbours*," I said pointedly.

Billy winced, knowing exactly what I was getting at. He'd been doing a lot of apologizing to me this week – saying sorry for Tuesday, saying sorry for saying dumb, laddish things without thinking. And, yeah, of course I'd forgiven him (that's what friends do) but I figured he still had to be punished. And his punishment was ... spending the morning babysitting Tor. It was only till Grandma – back from her holiday today – came round to take over, but I knew that spending a couple of hours alone with Spook-kid was going to feel like a ten-year prison sentence to Billy. Ha!

"Are you sure you couldn't just take Tor along to this rehearsal thing with you?" Billy grimaced at me hopefully.

"No way," I shook my head. "Boys aren't allowed to watch the class – *remember*?"

Billy blushed as red as the lipstick Glittery Gloria wore, which he got a pretty good look at on Tuesday night when she was yelling at him and the other lads to get lost...

I was Marie Antoinette, stepping up to the guillotine. I lowered my head down on to the hard wood block, knowing – dreading – that my time had nearly come...

"What a shame Kyra didn't want to do it!" I heard Rowan sigh.

OK, I wasn't Marie Antoinette about to get her head lopped off. I was Ally Love, about to get on stage and *die* of embarrassment, and that was practically just as bad from where I was standing...

"Well, it's probably just as well," I answered Rowan, with my eyes tight shut. "Kyra would have only got the giggles anyway."

I couldn't exactly feel annoyed with Kyra for bottling out of the belly-dancing show, not since she'd only been to one class, and not since she'd been such a brilliant friend to me by taking the blame for the "I love Alfie" doodles. ("Doesn't make any difference to me," she'd shrugged in her usual "so-what?" way the next day at school when I'd talked to her about it. "*I* don't care who people think I fancy.")

"Stay still, Ally!" Von suddenly ordered me, and who was I to argue?

Von was doing my make-up for the church-fête performance and I was doing my very best to stop my eyelids trembling as she drew long sweeps of black liner over them.

But it was hard to stop my eyelids trembling when the rest of me was trembling too. There were only a few minutes till we went on – the over-sixties tap-dancing troupe were just rat-tat-a-tapping out their last few steps on stage right now – and I wished I could run away, run up to Ally Pally, and hide in the bushes till it got dark. (I did that once before when I was nine and didn't want to go to the dentist. Only, then I was pretty inconspicuous, in my jeans and jumper. Today, with swooping black eyeliner, bare feet and belly, and a two-metre-wide silky purple veil, I might be a little more easily spotted.)

"Yeah, stay still, Ally!" I heard Rowan's voice come from behind me, then felt something cold and metallic being pulled around my forehead.

"What is it?" I asked, dying to open my eyes, or reach my hand up, but too frightened of Von telling me off while she did her make-up artist thing on me.

"It's an old necklace of Mum's with beads and coins on it," Rowan's voice explained. "I thought it would make your hair look less boring."

I bit the inside of my mouth to stop myself from yelping as she fastened the necklace to my "boring" hair with scratchy clips.

"OK ... that's you done!" Von announced.

Tentatively, I opened my eyes and checked that Von was speaking to me. It seemed so, even if she *was* examining me with that same dissatisfied expression I wore the time I tried to make a papier mâché sculpture, only I used too much water and ended up with a soggy, sticky pile of old paper instead of a prize-winning work of art.

"Ooh, Ally – you look great!" Rowan smiled at me, checking out the full effect.

I felt slightly cheered up, and less like a soggy, sticky pile of old paper, but then I remembered that Rowan always says stuff like that. And Von still wasn't exactly beaming at my gorgeousness.

"Come and have a look in the mirror!" said Rowan, grabbing my hand and leading me through the gaggle of other belly dancers, female Morris dancers (due on stage after us, and standing, for no reason I could work out, with ribbon-covered hula hoops), and leotard-wearing Yoga-cise class members (practising their bendy tricks).

There was a queue at the extra-wide, full-length mirror on the far wall, but the chattering Morris-dancing ladies quickly stopped adjusting their ribbon-covered hats after Von shot them one of her narrow-eyed Von looks (scary stuff), and made off, clutching their hula hoops nervously.

And then there I was, staring at my reflection – only it took me a while to recognize myself.

Actually, I looked at Von and Rowan first, standing on either side of me, disguised as total belly-dancing goddesses. Von was like a mini, Goth version of Glittery Gloria, dressed in a long, black chiffony skirt, with a black, lace crochet top pulled tight and tied under her boobs. Her long, black hair was glossy and straight, and she'd sprayed a strand on either side bright red, to match the red fringy shawl she'd tied around her hips. She was weighed down with silver jewellery, with heaps of ethnic, chunky bracelets on each wrist, and this intricate, Indian-looking necklace round her throat.

If Von was going for the minimal, dramatic look, Rowan was going for the full, ornate Christmas-tree effect. Everything sparkled with colour, from the spangly, tiny clips she'd dotted through her curly-wurly hair, to the pink sequins she'd sewn around the hem, sleeves and neckline of the cropped green top she was wearing. Her skirt, made from a ream of sari material she'd finally chosen last Saturday and spent the week making, was a bright but delicate pattern of pink, green, blue and yellow, covered with tiny, glinting squares of gold. Round her hip was a gold beaded shawl (a tenner in the Warehouse sale last year because all the beads were falling off it), while on her wrists were her multi-coloured metal bracelets, and round her waist and ankles she had tied fine, gold leather strips with tiny gold bells jingling from them (another home-made project she'd put together after buying up half the bead shop in Crouch End).

And me? Well, I didn't look anywhere near as glamorous as the other two, but I did look … kind of OK, in a that's-not-really-me-is-it? way. Rowan had rummaged in Mum's wardrobe that morning (once she'd stopped sighing at me for not being in any way organized), and come up with a long, flarey, purple, velvet skirt. On top, I'd pulled on a cropped black spaghetti-strap vest (borrowed from Linn's drawer – not that she knew it), and round my hips was a flowery black and purple scarf that I vaguely remembered seeing Mum once wearing in an old photo. Tied round my forehead, right above my swoopy black-rimmed eyes, was the heavy beaded necklace, and my tinkly anklet was fastened in place.

Weird, I decided, staring at this dressed up

stranger who only bore the weeniest, faintest resemblance to me. In fact, I only recognized myself by my boring, style-free brown hair and the little jelly belly on show above the waistband of my skirt. (Yuck.)

"Here! Don't forget your veils, girls!" said Glittery Gloria, handing us the three long, silky pieces of fabric we'd been rehearsing with all morning. (Von's was black with silver threads through it, Rowan's was bright pink, and mine was deep purple.)

"Thank you!" Rowan positively sparkled at our teacher.

This had to be my sister's finest moment, I decided. The only way someone could top this was to ask her to play the Sugar Plum Fairy in *The Nutcracker* next Christmas. (But to be honest, I don't think the Royal Ballet are quite ready to see the Sugar Plum Fairy done out in real fairy lights, which is how Rowan would probably want to play it.)

"And girls..." Gloria grinned at us, pulling a handful of something clinky from behind her back, "...just so you don't feel left out, I've looked out some spare coin belts for you to wear!"

Honestly, the way they gasped, you'd think someone had just told Von and Rowan that

Johnny Depp wanted to marry them *both*, like, this *week* or something. Quick as a flash, they grabbed a coin belt each (black for Von, natch; sky blue for Rowan and her Costume of Many Colours), tied them over their hip shawls and gave them an experimental, noisy shake.

Me? I felt about as confident about tying one of those belts on as I was of fastening myself into a *parachute*, for goodness' sake.

"There you go!" smiled Gloria, pulling the purple belt so tightly around me that I thought my bum would go numb. "Now come on, girls – we're on any second!"

Us. Just the three of us. We were going on first, to take up our positions at the back of the stage, arms aloft, veils floating, stomachs churning, while the rest of the group then trooped on and did their shimmery, shimmying thing.

Oh, no … oh, no … oh, no … I muttered silently in my head, as I followed Gloria, Rowan and Von to the stage entrance.

"Don't worry, Ally! It'll be all right!" Gloria immediately turned and smiled.

(Uh-oh – I hadn't been speaking in my head *after* all.)

"Yeah, and I'll whisper our moves to you!" Rowan tried to assure me. "And remember, Ally, it's not like there'll be anyone we know out there. It'll just be a bunch of old grannies and loads of women from the mother and toddler group that use the hall too!"

I didn't know if I totally believed that, but I didn't have time to panic any more – the twangy, Arabic music had started, and Von had taken her first steps out on to the stage, with Rowan following her. Gloria might have been giving me a warm, friendly smile, but the hand on my back forcing me forward felt very powerful indeed.

I was there. I was on stage. I'd found my spot, lifted my veil and turned to face the audience. Now there was only one thing to do – cross my eyes *just* enough so that the entire (huge) room went fuzzy and I couldn't make out any faces.

(There's a very fine art to doing this – cross them *too* much and it makes you go dizzy and look like a total *freak*.)

And for a while there, it worked. As the rest of the group hip-thrust their way on stage, I concentrated on swooping my hips around in a figure-eight shape, just like we'd been taught, never once focusing on anyone out there in Audience Land.

"The camel's coming next!" I heard Rowan whisper to me, as the music began to change.

And that was when I lost my concentration. Not with the camel – which I seemed to wriggle through OK – but with the eye-crossing. And it was then, when everything suddenly came into horrible, sharp focus, that I instantly saw a face I recognized.

And then another.

And then another.

And then some more.

"Back to the figure eight!" Rowan prompted me again, in a whisper.

So there I was, wobbling my hips and my jelly belly around for all to see: that all being Sandie, Kyra, Tor, Grandma, her boyfriend Stanley and – argh! – *Billy*. Somehow I hadn't expected any of them to come: Sandie and Kyra, 'cause they thought it was too silly; Grandma 'cause she didn't really approve of belly dancing; Tor and Stanley, 'cause of Grandma; and Billy, because of his peeping Tom trouble earlier in the week.

And even though I'd now absolutely and definitely decided that there was no difference between boy and girl mates, somehow it was *much* more mortifying knowing that Billy was out there watching me make a fool of myself. With Kyra and Sandie it didn't matter *nearly* so much.

"*Ungghhh…*" I groaned, immediately crossing my eyes again. Even though it was too late.

Then something made me uncross them – something that had just occurred to me.

I peered through the dancers shimmying away in front of me, and checked out my traitorous friends and family again.

No one was looking disapproving (i.e. Grandma); in fact Sandie, Tor, Stanley and even Grandma were clapping their hands in time to the music. And *no one* was sniggering (i.e. Kyra and Billy). Actually, Billy looked a bit shell-shocked; like a startled fish in a baseball cap, with his eyes wide and his mouth hanging open.

"And *twirl!*" I heard Rowan whisper urgently, as the music began fading out.

And so I twirled, losing sight of the audience and everyone I knew in it as I spun around with the silky, purple chiffon floating around me in the air.

And for a second, instead of feeling pretty stupid, I felt pretty … well, *pretty*, if you must know – jelly belly or not…

Chapter 20

THREE CHEERS (AND A CAMEL) FOR BILLY

"Wow!"

I couldn't believe it. I'd died and gone to dip heaven.

"What's all this for?" I asked Grandma, while I drooled over the kitchen table, which was heaving with cling-film-covered bowls of salsa, sour cream and guacamole – not to mention all the bags of nachos and kettle crisps.

"Well, since I've been away a while, I thought I'd better spoil you all – I know you won't have been eating properly!" Grandma smiled, as she slipped her jacket off, letting Stanley whisk it away from her.

Hmm – that was the first time I'd ever heard Grandma describe nachos as nutritious. Next thing she'd be telling me that doctors were recommending you eat a Cadbury's Creme Egg with every meal.

"Not that this is for tea," she corrected herself, pointing at the nibble-fest. "I've got some chicken and things in the oven for later, once your father and Linn are home from work. This … this is just so we can all celebrate your dance show!"

Aw, bless. Before Grandma went off on her holiday, she'd seemed kind of dubious about the notion of me and Rowan learning how to belly dance. But not only had she come along to watch us in action (and seen that it wasn't saucy after all, *and* that we weren't just wearing a couple of sequins glued to our boobs and not much else), she'd gone and laid this surprise on for us too.

And it was just as well she had – there were a whole load of mouths to feed, since Kyra, Sandie, Von and Billy had all trooped back to ours after our triumphant dancing debut. (OK – that's how Glittery Gloria described it. I'd call it a hideous ordeal that ended up being not so bad, but I guess that doesn't sound as inspiring.)

"Oh, Grandma! Thank you!" Rowan smiled, walking into the kitchen with Von in tow and clapping her hands in excitement. "This is so nice!"

"Well, come on, girls! Make yourself useful! Get the crisps in bowls and take all this through to the living room!" Grandma ordered us brusquely.

(She's never very good with compliments – Grandma's *way* too matter-of-fact for gushy stuff like that.)

"Can I help, Mrs Henderson?" Sandie asked her, hovering as Von, me and Rowan tore into sorting out the snacky stuff.

"Yes, please, Sandie – take some plates through, will you? And Billy – there's plenty of juice in the fridge. Can you take that out, and get some glasses too, please?"

"Uh-huh," Billy blinked, looking glad to have something to do.

Billy had said hardly anything after the show. He'd just trailed back to our house, silent as Tor, behind the rest of us, as we chatted and giggled and gossiped about how the whole performance had gone.

"Here – I'll get the glasses," I told him, not trusting Billy Stevenson with anything remotely breakable.

As everyone – apart from Billy and me – scurried through to the living room with bowls and plates, I felt suddenly shy. It was crazy to feel shy with someone I'd known for … *for ever*, but I was still a little spaced out at the idea of him watching me hip-thrusting about on stage.

"How come *you're* here?" I said, for the sake of something to say, as I piled the glasses on to a tray. "Since it's Saturday, won't *Anita* be waiting for you to meet her from work? You know, walk her home and give her a little *kiss* or something?"

Billy mumbled a mumble that I couldn't make out.

"Huh?"

"I *said*," he repeated, sounding awkward, "I've only held her hand – I haven't kissed her yet!"

I started to grin, and was just about to gear up to a marathon teasing session, when I remembered that he could tease me back pretty good after what he'd seen me do today. So I thought it was probably safer to change the subject.

"So how did babysitting Tor go this morning?"

"Yeah, OK – once I'd gone through and managed to drag him away from next door."

"What?" I said, innocently. "You mean, from the two—"

"OK! OK!" Billy interrupted, knowing I was going to remind him of the rotten name he'd called them. "Anyway, that vet bloke Michael was being really nice to Tor – talking to him about that freak of a fish he's got. But I did see him yawning when Tor wasn't looking…"

Poor Michael. I wondered if he realized he'd taken on an apprentice, whether he wanted one or not.

"So, what did you and Tor talk about when you were on your own back here?" I grinned, wishing

I could have been a fly on the wall for that. The vision of Tor saying nothing and Billy struggling for *anything* to say was pretty funny.

But how wrong could I be?

"Oh, yeah … I forgot about that," Billy blinked as a memory came back to him from the dim and distant past (i.e. this morning). "That secret stuff he was going on about? Y'know – that time he flipped out when I was round here? Well, he told me what it was."

OK. So Billy knew that I'd been wondering and worrying about this "secret stuff". And – oops! – it had just slipped his mind that Tor had confessed all. Proof, if you needed any more, that Billy's a berk.

"*What*? I mean, *how*?" I gabbled, putting the tray of glasses back down on the work surface before I dropped it.

"How? Well, I didn't know what to do with Tor, so I got desperate and asked to see his mice," Billy shrugged. "And then when we were looking at the little baby ones, he told me about this poem he wrote for school – 'The Mice Mum' or something."

"'The Mouse Mum'," I corrected him, remembering that hidden-away scrap of paper in the old margarine tub under the bed.

I hadn't told Billy about that – he'd been too busy lately, thinking about Anita and … well … being a berk.

"So," Billy continued, "he told me he'd got this homework assignment a while back, to write a poem about mums, so he'd written one all about Kylie."

"Kylie?" I frowned.

"Yeah, *Kylie*," Billy said matter-of-factly, as if he wondered how I could be so stupid. "The mouse that had the babies?"

"Oh," I shrugged, feeling a little like I'd failed Tor by not knowing the names of *all* the pets.

"So, he wrote this poem about Kylie having mice babies and he was really proud of it, only his teacher said he'd done it wrong – it was supposed to be about everyone's *own* mum."

"But I've seen the poem! It *was* about Mum!" I squeaked.

"You must have seen the second version – the one he rewrote. But the thing was, he didn't write about your mum the first time round because he's finding it pretty hard to remember her."

"He doesn't *remember* her? What are you on about? The poem's all about how he really misses her!"

"Yeah, and he does. Miss her, I mean," Billy

shrugged. "He told me he's really jealous of the other kids at school, all having mums to talk to. Specially some mate called Frankie—"

"Freddie," I corrected him, remembering the cosy, mumsy hug I saw Mrs Jackson give Tor when I went to pick him up after school that first day when Grandma was away.

"—yeah, Freddie or whatever."

"But how can he not remember Mum?" I protested. "Tor *loves* it when she sends us all those letters and cards and photos and stuff! He's even got the last picture she sent under his bed!"

"Yeah, 'cause he's trying really hard to remember what it felt like when she lived here," said Billy really slowly, as if I was being pretty dumb, not getting what he was trying to tell me. "Ally, Tor was only three when your mum left – he hasn't got the same memories of her as you and your sisters. And he's pretty messed up about it – he feels really guilty that he can't remember what she was like in real life."

Gulp.

Poor Tor – so that was his secret. He missed his mum, but he couldn't picture what she looked like first thing in the morning, all smiley and sleepy over the breakfast table, or smell the apple shampoo she always washed her hair in, or imagine how soft her cheek felt against your forehead when she cuddled you... And poor Tor didn't want to tell us that because he felt guilty.

The funny thing was, *I* was starting to find it harder and harder to remember all that stuff, she'd been gone so long. We all were, I think. God, I couldn't wait to tell Tor it was OK. And I couldn't wait to tell Dad and Linn and Rowan what was going on...

"Oh, and another secret –" Billy continued, glancing back out into the hall to check there was no one around.

There wasn't – there was only the sound of laughing and talking and some kind of Arabic-sounding music wafting through from the living room.

"– that stuff that you and your sisters and your dad always tell him about your mum doing charity work, and how she'll be back any day now?"

I nodded, lost for words.

"He thinks it's cobblers. He thinks *you* all believe it, but doesn't want to tell you *he* doesn't in case any of you get upset..."

Tor – what was he like? A whole heap smarter than me or any of my family gave him credit for, that was for sure. There we all were, keeping the truth from him, and he'd sussed it out for himself.

Then another thing suddenly struck me…

"Wait a minute," I frowned at Billy. "That is a *lot* of information. How did you get Tor to talk so much?!""

"Ally," said Billy wearily. "That took me about a *minute* to tell you. It took two *long* hours and a *lot* of stroking mice for Tor to tell me the same thing."

Now that made sense. I couldn't help but grin. In fact, a tidal wave of relief and giggles immediately splatted me right in the face, unbalancing me so much that I did something I shouldn't have – I grabbed my lovely, berky buddy Billy in a great big bear hug.

Oops. It was the sort of bear hug I'd give my dad, only Billy – if you hadn't noticed – isn't my dad. He's a boy, and you don't go around giving boys random bear hugs, unless they're your brother or your boyfriend or something.

I could feel the heat of his blush before mine started.

"Ally! Billy!" we heard Rowan shout through from the living room, as we leapt apart from each other.

"Unggg…" Billy grunted, like an embarrassed caveman.

"Umph," I grunted back, pink with shock at my stupid move.

"Hurry up!" Rowan yelled. "Come and see the video Stanley did!"

So *that's* why there was Arabic music coming from the living room. Without making eye contact, me and Billy went back to grabbing the juice cartons and picking up the tray of glasses as if nothing had happened.

But before we got to the doorway of the kitchen, a crimson-red Billy stopped me by turning and saying something else.

"And, um, there's something else..." Billy mumbled, swivelling his baseball cap back to front and not looking me in the eye.

"What?" I asked, feeling my own eyes go walk-about rather than settle on him.

"When you were doing your dance thing today," he muttered. "You were, y'know, good. Really good. I mean, you looked ... well, *brilliant*."

What – me and my jelly belly looked brilliant? I didn't know whether to laugh or blush, so I said something stupid instead.

"What – not like a wobbly rhinoceros?"

Billy stared at me, confused, and then both of us stopped blushing and went back to what we do best – sniggering like a couple of kids. The way best friends do.

"Oi!" we heard Rowan hurry us up.

And with that, we did what we were told and hurried up, through to the living room, in time to see the strangest sight: and I'm not talking about the vision of our whole class shimmying around on the stage (and on the TV screen). It was just that I'd never in a million years have expected my staid and sensible grandma to be wiggling around the coffee table in a jangling coin hip belt, along with her white-haired sixty-something-year-old boyfriend, wearing the very purple belt I'd danced in earlier.

"We forgot to give these back to Gloria!" Rowan giggled, brandishing a third hip belt. "Here you go, Billy!"

"No! I can't!" Billy yelped, clutching his two cartons of juice tight as Rowan slithered her hands around his waist and tied it on.

"If you can wear a bra on your head, Billy Stevenson, you can wear a coin belt round your hips!" Kyra bellowed at him, grabbing the cartons out of his hands, while Sandie hid her face and dissolved into giggles.

"Come on!" I laughed at Billy. "I'll show you how to do the camel!"

"What?!" yelped Billy. "*Noooooo...*"

See my big sister Linn? She thinks she lives in a madhouse at the best of times, but when she walked in the door that evening, she must have thought she'd taken a wrong turn and walked into a circus tent or something. I mean, our house is always mental, but finding nine people and two dogs doing a hip-thrusting conga line through the hallway must have blown her mind.

Specially when we forced her to join in...

Anyway, that's it – got to go. It's my turn to have a Girls' DVD Night, and I've got to sort out the nibbly bits before Sandie and Chloe and everyone arrive. *Yes*, there'll be nachos, and *yes*, I'll be eating some – only I'll try not to eat my whole body weight in them, just so the jelly belly doesn't get any bigger. Not that it bugs me so much now – not after I saw all the jelly bellies in the belly-dancing class and realized that it's kind of *normal* for girls to have them.

Unless you're Kate Moss, of course, but then to stay *that* thin, I bet she can *never* know the sheer joy of nachos and dip – and that's just *too* sad.

All for now :c)

PS I never did go back to belly-dancing classes, even if Billy did think I looked – ahem – "brilliant". Rowan and Von still go and still love it, but all the glitter and tinkly stuff was just a bit too girlie for me. And, if you want to know the truth, every time I tried to shimmy, it just made me want to wee. Maybe I've got a weak bladder or something.

PPS So, that quizzy question: can boys and girls truly be just friends? Well, if I was an Agony Aunt on a magazine advice page, I'd say absolutely and definitely *yes*. My only tip is, DON'T go giving your boy buddy a bear hug, even by accident – that makes things very, *very* confusing. And let's face it, boys' brains are confused enough as it is. (I'd better not say that to Billy or I'll get another Chinese burn.)

PPPS Anyone want a baby mouse? We've got plenty looking for good homes...

Also by Karen McCombie

Stella Etc.

To: You
From: Stella
Subject: Stuff

Hi there!

You'd think it would be cool to live by the sea with all that sun, sand and ice cream. But, believe me, it's not such a breeze. I miss my best mate Frankie, my terror twin brothers drive me nuts and my mum and dad have gone daft over the country dump, sorry, "character cottage", that we're living in. I'm bored, and I'm fed up with being the new girl on the block. Still, I quite fancy finding out more about the mysterious, deserted house in Sugar Bay. And what's with the bizarre old lady who feeds fairycakes to seagulls. . .?
Catch up with me (and my fat, psychic cat!) in the Stella Etc. series.
LOL

stella
XXX

Want to know more. . .?

Check out Karen's super-cool website!

karenmccombie.com

For behind-the-scenes gossip on Karen's very own blog,
fab competitions and photo-galleries,
join her website of loveliness now!